A PEACE OF MIND IS BETTER THAN HALF A MAN

RUTH HAMPTON

RUTH HAMPTON WRITES, LLC

TABLE OF CONTENTS

How Come?

"Be completely humble and gentle; be patient, bearing one another in love. Make every effort to keep the unity of the Spirit through the bond of peace."

Ephesians 4:2-3 (King James Version Bible)

This fictional novel is dedicated to victims and their loved ones associated with domestic violence or those who may be or have been in a toxic relationship. Please do not suffer in silence. You are not alone. If you feel you are in an abusive or toxic relationship, then please seek professional help immediately.

If there are any abusers and/or victims of domestic violence who may be suffering from or dealing with mental illness. Please do not suffer in silence. You are not alone. Seek professional help if you are suffering from and/or been diagnosed with mental illness .

Disclaimer: Ruth Hampton, the author, is not of the medical profession and does not claim to be; therefore, you are not obligated to take her advice...be persuaded by your own mind.

ACKNOWLEDGEMENT

~Firstly, I want to thank God the Father, God the Son, and the Holy Spirit for giving me the gift of being a writer and on becoming a self-published author.

~Secondly, I want to thank my children (Joshua and Jasmyne) and my grandkids (Alayziah, Ma'Kiyah, Lorenzo, and Lamarco) for being my strongest supporters and reasons behind my authorship. Praying to leave this legacy for them.

~Thirdly, I thank my parents Elijah Hampton, Sr.(deceased) and Mae Covington-Hampton for birthing me and giving me their personality traits: Dad (humor, ambition, open mindedness, happy-go-lucky attitude, friendliness; leadership); Mom (strong faith, humor, leadership, patience, ambition, friendliness).

~Fourthly, I thank my siblings, nieces, and nephews for sticking with me and always having my back!

~Finally, I thank my special friends who stick by me listening to my cries, complaints, defeats, and successes without judgment.

ABOUT RUTH HAMPTON

Ruth Hampton was raised in a small, rural town known as Benson ("Mule City"), NC As a youngster, she enjoyed writing poetry and later, research essays in college while pursuing her Master of Arts in Teaching Special Education Degree from UNC-Charlotte. Go Niner Nation!

She continues to reside in North Carolina while working as an educator in special education and fulfilling her dream as a self-published author.

Ruth's sources of inspiration and testimony for writing are brought on by her personal experiences from domestic violence and toxic relationships.

One day Ruth prayed to God for deliverance from hating the past detrimental situations that she found herself in and erroneous decisions she made to have and/or keep a man (twice). Yes; even as a Christian, she fell into depression and anxiety. Later, wound up in therapy and on medication—the best decision ever made—without shame or guilt. Ruth believes your mind deserves a tune up just like your car. If ignored over a period of time, it will break down from all the wear and tear.

Remember, the scripture declares, "But when Jesus heard that, he said unto them, They that be whole need not a physician, but they that are sick (Matthew 9:12)." She is a firm believer that God + therapy + medication(if necessary)

= healing. God continued to bring healing when HE told her: "A person has a right to love who and what they want. He just didn't choose you." You might be surprised what you—the wife or significant other—can be left in the dust for besides a mistress. Whether it's power, control, lover of money, alcohol, and/or drugs.

Just like God gives us a chance and a choice to serve him of our own free will, so it is with humans and marriage. It's okay to forgive and let that person go without staying bitter or holding grudges. You do not have to prove anything to anyone when you forgive. God knows and that is all that matters. Keep moving forward now with a peace of mind; embarking on your own journey with God. Your journey is not going to mimic another's; so no explanation is needed as to what yours (journey) may seem like to others.

Though life tosses numerous curveballs, unexpected hills, and deep-trodden valleys towards her, God blesses Ruth to overcome and continue striving to accomplish her passions; her loves—writing and authorship. God has instilled an immeasurable portion of faith within Ruth that is "like a tree planted by the rivers of water, that bringeth forth his fruit in his season; his leaf also shall not wither and whatsoever he doeth shall prosper (Psalm 1:3 KJV)."

INTRODUCTION

TOXIC RELATIONSHIPS

Toxic relationships can be extremely damaging to one's mental and emotional health and overall well-being. These types of relationships often start out great but quickly spiral into something toxic and dangerous. Signs of these types of relationships include but are not limited to: constant fighting, gaslighting, and manipulation. It's important to recognize these signs and take action to remove oneself from the relationship before it becomes too detrimental. Seek help from a trusted support network if you find yourself in a toxic relationship.

One of the biggest challenges can be recognizing when a relationship has become toxic and knowing how to address it. It's important to establish healthy communication habits early on in a relationship to prevent toxic behavior from taking root.

Clarification of: Fighting?: Fighting in a toxic relationship is never easy. It can be physical violence (hitting or pushing) and/or verbal abuse (demeaning each other). It can feel like a constant battle where both partners are trying to gain the upper hand. Mainly the dominant of the two wanting control.

This type of relationship can take a toll on a person's mental health and self-esteem. Despite this, it can also be difficult to break away from the relationship. Why? Perhaps, the toxic partner may have a hold on or control of the other person. Fighting in a toxic relationship is an incredibly disheartening and an emotionally draining experience. It can leave one feeling trapped, hopeless, and lost. The constant bickering, arguing, and hurtful words can lead to depression and anxiety.

Verbal abuse in a toxic relationship looks like a lot of different things. It can be as subtle as snarky comments and backhanded compliments or as overt as screaming and name-calling. Regardless of the form it takes, verbal abuse is never acceptable in a healthy relationship. Often concealed behind a façade of love and care, the abuser uses verbal abuse as a means of control and domination over their partner. It can cause serious emotional harm, destroy self-esteem, and even lead to physical abuse. Despite this, many individuals stay in toxic relationships due to fear, guilt, or a mistaken belief that they can change their partner. Or, if they pray hard enough or long enough, they will change.

Change happens when one is willing to admit he/she has a problem. Then, seek professional help or counseling to deal with those intense or strong emotions that spark at the 'drop of a hat.'

Gaslighting?: This is when one person tries to convince the other that their perceptions of reality are incorrect, often leading the victim to doubt their own sanity. It can be difficult to recognize gaslighting when you're in the midst of it, but it's important to be aware of this tactic and seek professional help if you suspect it's happening to you. Remember, you are not crazy or imagining things - gaslighting is a real and harmful form of abuse.

Manipulation?: One form of manipulation is using guilt to control the victim, often by making them feel responsible for the abuser's behavior. Additionally, abusers may isolate their partners from friends and family, making it harder for them to seek support or leave the relationship.

If you feel you are in an abusive relationship or need help with mental illness, please seek help immediately.

Disclaimer: Ruth Hampton, the author, is not of the medical profession and does not claim to be; therefore, you are not obligated to take her advice...be persuaded by your own mind.

INTERPRETATION
AUTHOR'S OPINION

Disclaimer: This is the author's interpretation or opinion of what is believed to be "a piece of or half a man." The author's interpretation or opinion is not meant to shame, slander, or slay a man's character but hopefully the examples within the books will point out ways an abuser or one who may not realize he's abusive (without being physical) can/will change his behavior as pleasing to God.

"a piece of a man" or "half a man: an unstable and/or insecure male who does not and/or may refuse to follow the leadership of God. He simply brings no spiritual value or harmonious equality to the relationship, instead he instills fear to dominate and/or control his spouse or significant other.

WORD of GOD: I Peter 3:7; 1Corinthians 6:9-11 and 7:2-5; Hebrews 13:4; Genesis 2:18-24; Ephesians 5:22-33

When you read the scriptures concerning marriage, God styled the marriage as the church. God is supposed to be the head of human life. HE meant for the man to be head of the household and left scripture and guidelines for him to lead his family spiritually, emotionally, and honorably. You will not find in God's Word that a woman should be: (a) re-raised as a child by her husband or significant other; (b) used as a punching bag or door mat; and/or (c) spoken to as a regurgitated-filled garbage can.

PROLOGUE

Rayna stood and said, "Well, I just came to pack a bag and head on back."

"Why don't you stay with us and go back tomorrow?"

"Nah, Grandma, I want to see the twins as much as possible because when I get back." she paused and dropped her head, "when I get back, I got so much to do. I still have a job, you know." Wiping away tears, she continued, "And I need to renovate my entire house. I don't want no part of Elliot around me."

David mumbled, "Or you could sell it."

"No, Granddad, I'm not going to let him take what I worked so hard to build!"

Grandma Flo squeezed her tightly and said, "You fight for your life, child. It's yours. God gave it to you and with Him backing you, you gone be alright. You gone be just fine."

After the hugs and goodbyes, she went home and packed a bag. Upon leaving, she thought she saw a glimpse of Carol and James in the neighborhood walking alongside a handsome young man—as if they were helping him.

Ray-Ray thought to herself, "What they doing over here? And who is that with them? I'll find out after the funeral."

CHAPTER 1

AT DEATH'S DOORS

"Ray-Ray! Can you hear me? C'mon, sweetie. It's me...Sierra! Open your eyes, girl!" Sierra begins shaking her and tapping her face.

I want to wake up but, my eyes refuse to cooperate! I can barely breathe. My body aches all over. I feel blood trickling down my face and flowing into my mouth. Tastes salty—feels warm. Overfilling my throat like a boat sinking deeper into the sea. Choking me. I—I'm going to—vomit!

"Help me!" my mind cries out. I want to scream, but I can't find my voice! It's gone!

There's someone standing over me. I can't see clearly. I don't recognize the voice. Those NOISY sirens!

Wiggling fingers and toes, I can't move! My body's numb.

Someone's crying hysterically as one of the paramedics sounds annoyed with her. "Ma'am, step aside, please. We need to load her on the gurney."

A man's voice was giving police an update on what ensued as the paramedics lifted my body onto the stretcher and whisked me into the ambulance.

It sped down the highway and felt as though it was about to turn over.

"Oh no! The baby! My baby! I hope it's alright!"

Suddenly, the screeching tires came to an abrupt stop. We must be at the hospital. I can hear the paramedics talking. Trying to speak in a low tone. "Man, this one took a grave beating. She looks pretty bad. I don't understand how a man can do this to a woman. I sure would like to get my hands on him."

"Well, they gotta find him first," a female voice said. "Word is that he's kinda crazy. I hope they ready for him when they catch him."

My heart dropped. Too many thoughts running through my head now. I feel dizzy. Too many bright lights in here. My eyes hurt so bad.

"Help me!" My mind is still screaming, but my mouth won't speak.

"Hurry!" the doctor stepped in. "We need to get x-rays to make sure there's no internal bleeding and to check for broken bones. She looks like she's lost quite a lot of blood."

Mama's trembling voice ringing out, "Baby girl! Oh, my baby! God, please, don't...!

James comforted her, "It's okay, sweetheart, I got you." He reached over and touched my arm. "You're going to be okay, baby girl. We are praying for you."

"Ray-Ray! It's Sierra. Benjamin and I are here. You're going to be okay, Ray! I love you, sis!"

"Oh Lord! My baby. God, please save Ray-Ray, Lord." Grandma pleaded and continued, "Ray-Ray, David and the police out looking for that heathen...Elliot! Don't worry. They gone catch his behind. He betta pray when they do. God got you Ray-Ray. No worries!"

They whisked me to radiology as the nurse was giving the doctor the details about what happened.

Sierra said, "Carol, I called Raymond. He and Tasha on the way. Hilda Mae gone stay with the twins."

"Thanks, Sierra. I didn't feel up to calling him."

"I kinda figured that." Sierra gave Carol a hug and quickly returned to Benjamin's arms.

Carol was still in shock. Her small-framed body was shaking with fear as James pulled her into his tight, muscular chest. His strong, robust hands caressing her tiny shoulders as he gently kissed the warm, salty tears rolling down her soft cheeks. "I'm right here, babe."

Thinking of his own familial loss while holding her, James wept in silence.

"CODE BLUE! I REPEAT, CODE BLUE!"

CHAPTER 2

MORE ARGUMENTS

"Slow down, Raymond. I know you're upset, baby, but you need to let me drive." Tasha said nervously.

"Don't tell me how to drive, Tasha!" Raymond shouted. "My baby might die because of that maniac!"

Tasha turned and stared out the window and didn't respond. Her eyes swelled with tears. She knew when to be silent. And she wanted no more arguing between them. It seems that is all they've been doing lately ever since Raymond found out Carol was marrying James.

Raymond said calmly, "I'm sorry for yelling at you, Tasha. Forgive me?"

"No problem, Raymond. I understand." She glanced at him attempting a cordial smile.

He reached for her hand on the seat and held it. "I'm going to pull over baby and let you drive. You're right."

Raymond stopped at the nearest convenient store and hopped in the back seat.

"Why are you sitting back there?"

"Tasha, why you gotta ask "why? I'm tired and want to take a nap before we get there. Is that okay with you? Stop nagging me!"

Angered and annoyed by Raymond's tone of voice, Tasha vehemently says, "Seriously! I'm a "nagger" now? You know what, Raymond, it may not be the right time to bring this up, but we need to go to marriage counselling."

"I already told you that I ain't going. Everyday just ain't gone be sunny, Tasha, and you need to get that through your thick skull."

"Well, you the one that's purposely causing all these clouds in our marriage right now. Sittin' up here pining away over your ex!"

"Okay, so you holding on to that. Have you forgotten she's getting married to that weeping widower?"

"Nah, but I think you have. You jealous jerk!" And Tasha rolled her eyes while trying not to cry.

"Just drive and get us to the hospital so I can see Ray-Ray! I'm gonna get some sleep. Wake me when we get there, please."

"I don't know; I might have your precious Carol to do it." Tasha snapped back.

Raymond didn't respond. Tasha was furious and sped off; squalling tires; leaving black, wavy skid marks behind.

Tears streaming down her face, Tasha began to reflect on those sullen moments of arguments since they found out Carol and James were getting married.

She knew it was hard on the kids and Aunt Hilda Mae playing referee and trying to remain unbiased. Deep down in her heart...in the pit of her stomach, Tasha felt she was losing Raymond to a woman who didn't even want him. Or does she? Does Carol still have feelings for Raymond?

They finally pulled into the driveway of the hospital. Benjamin and Sierra were outside getting some fresh air; holding each other tightly.

Raymond jumped out of the car almost before it came to a halt, "Where's Carol? How is she?"

CHAPTER 3

SUSPECT IN SIGHT

"Over here, Lieutenant! I found something!" An officer yelled as he saw a bloody change of clothing by a dumpster in an alley near the crime scene. It was a matching pair of black sweatpants and jacket.

"Quick! Bag and tag it for evidence," Lt. John Kerr shouted. He turned to David and said, "So, tell me more about this guy we're hunting."

"Well, he's definitely crazy. His name is Elliot Nolan. We believe that he killed his aunt and three cousins, but no one could prove it. He beat my granddaughter, Rayna, nearly to death."

"Does anyone know where he may be going? Does he have a weapon?" asked Lt. Kerr.

"Um, he's armed and dangerous. I have no idea where he's trying to get to. Elliot's very familiar with traveling internationally; so, he might be trying to leave the country. I would set up officers at the airport, of course." David's phone started buzzing. "Oh! Please make sure several officers are at the hospital. I have a feeling Elliot may come after my granddaughter first."

"No problem. I'm on it." Lt. Kerr reassured him.

Answering the call, David said abruptly, "I need to get to the hospital. Please keep me posted, and y'all be careful."

"Okay, man. I'm sorry about your granddaughter." Lt. Kerr gathered some officers, and they had the forensics team scout for prints on and around the dumpster in the alley.

David was walking to his car, but felt chills as he reached for his door. He briskly turned...looking to the left...to the right. Looking up, he saw a slim figure in the distance atop a building. The figure seemed to salute him and then run.

"Hey!" David yelled out, "Lt. Kerr! Run! I see him on top of that old factory building! C'mon!"

Sirens blaring! Feet trotting; heavy breathing; tires screeching! Officers shouting out throughout the allies. Elliot ran down the fire escape. In and out of allies. Until...

Lt. Kerr crying out, "Halt! This is the Police! Hands in the air!" Elliot turned around slowly with a smile upon his face. His bloody knuckles grasping a 38 in his right hand down by his side. "Drop your weapon!" Lt. Kerr warned. Some officers could be heard trotting in and out of alleyways in the distance. Police cars forming blockades throughout the exits.

The man glares at the lieutenant and doesn't drop the weapon. Instead he shoots and quickly dodges down an alley but not without getting shot in the left arm by Lt. Kerr. "I'm hit! I'm hit! Officer down! Get him! Please!" Lt. Kerr called for help in writhing pain with blood spewing from his right upper thigh as officers began to gather at the scene. Elliot, on the move, was gone before they arrived.

David could see the figure dressed in black running faster and faster...like a track star! Stop, Elliot!" David tried to keep up.

Suddenly, David had to stop as his legs were falling from under him and his chest tightened. Barely able to breathe; hassling for air. He felt faint but could see the man stop and gaze at him for a brief moment. The culprit was wearing a black hoodie with matching jogging pants. There was blood dripping from the left side of the man's black jacket. Then he ran off looking back with a sinister grin on his face reminding David, "I'm gone kill that ho if it's the last thing I do."

"Elliot!" David whispered before passing out.

Chapter 4

Hospital Drama

"C'mon, Tasha!" Raymond snatched her by the hand and went into the hospital. Tasha looked back at the curious bystanders...disheartened and embarrassed by his actions.

Once inside, Raymond asked, "How's Ray-Ray?"

"Hi, Raymond," Grandma Flo rushed over to hug him, "Ray-Ray's in pretty bad shape. We're praying and waiting for the doctor to give us a report." She turned to Tasha and said, "Hey baby, you and Raymond can sit over here."

Grandma Flo felt the tension between them and purposely seated them near her away from Carol and James. Tasha immediately took her advice while Raymond walked over to Carol and James.

"Um, excuse me," Raymond said...ignoring James' presence. "Carol, can I have a word with you? I need..."

James interjected, "Whatever you think you have to say to my wife, you can say in front of me, Brother Raymond."

In a jealous rage, Raymond said angrily, "Wife? Since when?" Looka here, this is my and Carol's daughter; not yours. I want to talk to my daughter's mother...alone!"

Carol quickly turned to Raymond, "James and I got married at the Justice of Peace a few days ago. It was a private affair. I figured your Aunt Hilda Mae would've told you since Mama mentioned it to her."

Tasha was no longer in tears. She now looked at Raymond with a smirk on her face. Benjamin and Sierra were looking on in dismay and couldn't help but feel sorry for Raymond. They thought he knew.

Raymond couldn't say anything at this point and stormed off like an embarrassed teenager. Grandma Flo got up and ran after him. Tasha just sat back and thought, "Yeah, James gained a wife, and you might be getting ready to lose yours, Raymond."

Benjamin and Sierra walked over to talk to James and Carol. "Dad, I'm proud of you for standing up for your wife. I ain't gone put up with that from any man trying to step to my good thang."

Sierra chimed in, "And I sho' ain't gone stand by and let someone snatch my "Mr. Right" either." Without hesitation, she and Benjamin's hands clasped together like intertwined vines wrapped around a fence post.

Feeling sorry for James being caught in the middle, Carol said, "James, I apologize, honey. I don't know what's wrong with Raymond. I wanna go talk to Tasha. I feel bad for her."

Kissing her softly on the cheek, James reassured her that he was okay and an apology wasn't necessary.

Carol knew how Tasha felt and went over to her.

Tasha saw her coming and immediately felt defensive. "Listen, you can have him. I can't fight for someone that doesn't want me."

"Tasha, I don't want Raymond. I will always love him for giving me such a beautiful, wonderful daughter. I love James so much and feel he is my soulmate. I came over to let you know that I'm not your problem nor your enemy. I know what you're going through. I want us to be friends, Tasha. Please? "

Tasha began to cry. "I would like that Carol. It's just that Raymond and I..." Sierra came over with some tissue. "I may have to take the kids and leave Raymond if he doesn't..."

Carol tried to calm her. "Don't make any rash decisions based on emotions right now, Tasha. Maybe y'all can go to counseling. He's just confused and got a lot going on."

To put her mind at ease, Sierra said, "Yeah, I know some great marital counselors that could probably help you guys. If you want, I can give you the name of the one that Benjamin and I are going to."

"But no counselor can change the love of a person's heart and mind that's made up for someone else. And I don't want to waste any more of my time in this marriage. If Raymond chooses me over his past relationship with you, Carol, then it only means I'll be second. I'll never be first...no matter what I do or how much counseling we get. I don't want a piece of or a half of a man. I deserve better than this. Now, I'll go to counseling for my mental health and my children's sake."

Carol and Sierra hugged her. "If there's anything I can do to help you, Tasha, let me know. I really want to be your friend," Carol said again. She and Sierra walked back over to James and Benjamin.

Grandma Flo went outside to talk to Raymond. "Have you lost your mind, Raymond!" Grandma Flo scolded him as though he were a child. "You got a good wife in there who's watching you get upset over a woman that don't belong to you and ain't coming back to you. You betta fix it with Tasha."

"I can't! I'm still in love with her, Ms. Florence. I don't know what I'm going to do. I think she married James too fast. And I believe she still loves me too."

"Oh shut up, Raymond, with your 'woulda, coulda, shoulda! And no she's not...Carol is in love with James!"

"Nah! She thinks she is, but I know her better than anyone, Ms. Florence. She just puttin' on a act."

"Boy, you sure are stuck on stupid. Have you asked yourself 'why you're still in love with her after all these years? Notice that you didn't bring up these feelings until Carol got with James? Honestly, I think you're just envious of them. You need to quit this foolishness and talk to your wife."

"What for? She knows I have feelings for Carol."

"Well, I hate it! That's two good women you've lost."

An ambulance pulled up and rushed past Raymond and Grandma Florence.

Dr. Knight came out to give the family an update about Ray-Ray's condition.

CHAPTER 5

REAPING DAY

Sirens were blaring all over town. Blustering winds sent flurries of raindrops tapping and dancing on the streets and cars. All Elliot thought about was finding a place where he could bind up his wound, rest, and get out of those wet clothes. He needed to get out of Sumnerfield—regroup.

"I'm gone get that ho before I go to Costa Rica. You'll have your part in the lake, Rayna...my lake! I will have my revenge on all of y'all!"

Elliot's left arm was throbbing now. He was losing a lot of blood and needed to take care of this wound. His duffle bag weighed him down as it was packed with clothes, money, guns, and ammo.

Parked at *Townsend's Liquor Shop*, Elliot quickly helped himself to the bed of an old, dented pickup truck and pulled the dirty, worn-out tarp over himself. Soon a man came out whistling and placed a heavy crate on top of the tarp. "Ouch!" Elliot groaned in silence.

The man climbed in and blasted the radio to some country tunes. The old pickup rolled over potholes; bouncing those bottles in the crate up and down on Elliot's arm. Blood continuously spurted.

Elliot felt really tired. He started drifting off to sleep when the tires came to a screeching halt. The man hopped out of the truck and grabbed the crate.

Waiting until the coast was clear, Elliot peeped from under the tarp and noticed the driver was a tall, young, Caucasian male in a cowboy hat with his hair pulled back in a ponytail. Looked like an elite athlete at some point. Then Elliot recognized the shabby-looking, dilapidated yellow house. This "hole-in-the-wall"—liquor house—seemed familiar to him. Charlestown!

Disoriented, he sat on the edge of the truck wheezing; trying to catch his breath. The heavy downpour seemed to blind him as he checked his surroundings.

"Am I really in Charlestown?" he said to himself. He stood up and stumbled backwards.

Looking around, he walked hurriedly down a long gravel path in a wooded area off the main highway at the edge of town. "Thank God," he whispered. There was a small, cozy-looking cabin hidden near the train tracks. A dim porch light was on. Elliot took out the 38 and crept towards the cabin. He didn't see a car in the driveway but heard music playing inside; a familiar song—God's Alright Wit Me." A well of tears streamed down Elliot's face as the song played. Dark memories flooded his mind to that stormy night during his childhood when he lost his parents in the automobile accident. He looked towards Heaven. "Man, I miss you guys so much!"

Bleeding profusely, Elliot felt weak. He was hungry, wet, cold, and sleepy. With his gun in his hand, he got ready to knock on the door. WHOO! WHOO! The train whistled. It was moving slowly down the tracks. Elliot became frightened and hid behind a tall oakwood tree. He saw a tall, slim figure with a small sack jump from the train. The man limped to the cabin and went inside.

"What in the world?" Elliot muttered to himself.

Shaking with fear and from the coldness of the torrential rain, Elliot convinced himself that he would have to bum-rush the man once he knocks on the door. Holding his gun in his right hand, Elliot banged on the door.

The man jumped up, "Who is it?" No one answered. When he flung open the door, Elliot charged at him like a bull seeing red. There was a scuffle and three shots later...thud! The limp body fell heavily to the floor.

Breathing slowly, Elliot didn't feel angry anymore; he felt relieved. Lying on the cold, wooden floor with his gun still in his hand, he looked up at the man's familiar yet disfigured burnt face and mumbled, "Damon? But...How...how?"

"How what, Elliot? Damon asked angrily. "You did this to me! I tried to save those people from the fire that you set."

"But...but, they killed my brother, Elijah and covered it up."

"Well, how'd you get shot before you got here?" Damon was curious as he saw that 'life' was about to take it's flight from Elliot.

Barely able to breath now, Elliot continued to speak. "Man, I messed up. I tried to kill, Rayna, my wife. The cops are after me."

"So fate has finally come for you. I wish I coulda been around to stop her from marrying you, Elliot."

"You ain't no better. Still stealing, thief? She ain't gone talk to you no way! Scar face!" Blood sputtered from his mouth.

"Yeah but I ain't no murderer, bro. Besides, I don't need to steal no more. I got enough cash to get my 'scar face' fixed."

Looking into his solemn eyes, Damon saw death written all over Elliot's face. He felt sorry for him. "Man, I apologize. I mean, even though we are foster brothers, I love you like a real one. You should've told me who you were when you knocked on the door. I wouldn't shot you. Why didn't you say your name?"

But Elliot couldn't answer him. He was gone to join his real family.

Damon's right arm was spewing blood from Elliot's gun blast which didn't seem to phase him. After cleaning and wrapping his bloody arm, he looked through Elliot's duffle bag and took about three bundles of cash. He stashed the cash under the floorboards alongside the small sack he had taken from the train.

Setting down the duffle bag near Elliot's body by the door, he took the tourniquet off and put it in the garbage disposal. Looking back at Elliot, he said, "I'm sorry bro."

He picked up the cell phone and called the police. "Hey, I'm at 2-5-9 Elmway Road. Off the main highway. I just killed an intruder and, I've been shot." He hung up the phone.

Chapter 6

Good News; Bad News

Everyone rushed towards Dr. Knight at once with looks of panic and worry. "How is Ray-Ray, Doctor?"

"Well, she will pull through. But I'm afraid, she lost the baby. Rayna's going to need a lot of care for a long while; I can't..."

"Baby?! What baby!?" Grandma Flo sounded baffled.

"Oh, you didn't know? She was about 6 weeks pregnant. Rayna has a concussion, broken left wrist, broken left jawbone along with some missing teeth, broken right collarbone, busted right eardrum, eyes swollen shut, and multiple bruises on her body. That guy did a number on her."

Carol jumped in, "When can we see her, Doctor? I'm her mother."

"And I'm her father," Raymond said proudly and went to stand on the other side of Carol opposite James.

"I'm her stepfather, Pastor James Nolan" as he reached out to shake Dr. Knight's hand and gently pulled Carol to his side away from Raymond.

"Well, you all can see her tomorrow morning. Two at a time, please. She's heavily sedated right now. She'll probably be in here for about two weeks or more. We want to make sure that she will be alright."

Sierra was crying, "Is she going to be like...you know?"

"You mean physically incapacitated? Yes, for only a little while. But mentally, she has a long recovery. It seems like she already has a strong support system though."

"She sure does, Doctor." James said as he glared at Raymond.

Seemingly frustrated, Raymond's face tightened as he clenched his fist. He felt as though he were going into a rage.

Tasha stood afar in the distance—watching. Sadly, she knows what she has to do now.

Police officers started swarming in. Benjamin recognized one of them from his high school days. "Hey, Axel Young! What's going on, man?"

"Hey, Benjamin Murphy! It's good to see you, bro.

"You? A cop! I can't believe it! You know what I mean?" And they both laughed.

"C'mon, man. The past is the past. I grew up and put away childish things. I'm married with two kids." Officer Young took out his wallet and showed Benjamin pictures of his wife and kids.

"That's what's up, man. I'm proud of you. So, what brings you here?"

"Well, our Lieutenant was shot, and a private eye had a heart attack chasing a suspect. We were told to guard a lady named, Rayna Nolan..."

Realizing that he was talking too much, Axel said, "Sorry, man, I gotta go."

"Wait!" Benjamin pleaded. "Rayna's my sister-in-law. Her parents are over there. Have you...?"

"I've said too much already, friend." Axel walked over to talk with the Doctor and Rayna's parents.

"CODE BLUE! CODE BLUE!" came over the intercom and Dr. Knight ran to the back to help out.

Axel looked worried and said, "I hope that private eye and Lt. Kerr are okay."

Grandma Flo ran to him and said, "What did you say?"

"Lt. Kerr and some private eye—an older gentleman."

She clutched her heart, "Oh no! David?" Her mind whizzed back to her precious Harold's passing. She cried uncontrollably. "Please, Lord, not again!"

Axel comforted her. "He suffered a heart attack I think ma'am. He was chasing a suspect."

"Elliot!" she screamed.

"Calm down, Sister Florence!" James reminded her.

Tears strolling down her cheeks to her neck, she said sharply, "I know, Pastor, but he hurt Ray-Ray, caused my David harm, and killed my great-grandbaby!"

Sierra brought her some tissue, hugged her, and sat next to Benjamin. "Officer, did y'all get the suspect?"

Disappointingly, Axel said, "No ma'am. He got away. But we'll get him...um Ms....uh?"

Dr. Knight came back out hurriedly. "I'm sorry for leaving like that but duty called."

"Doctor, is David okay?"

"Oh, Mama!" Carol cried. She thought of Mr. David as a father to her since her Dad passed.

Dr. Knight looked confused. "I'm sorry ma'am, but I can only discuss that information with his family. I have to get the nurse to notify Ms. Florence Jennings, his fiancée."

"Excuse me, Doctor, but I'm Florence Jennings."

Axel stood up as he saw the paramedics bring in Lt. Kerr who gave him a wave to signal that he was going to be okay. Axel smiled and turned to Benjamin, "It sure was good to see you, man." Then he glanced at Sierra and told Benjamin, "She's a beauty; you're a lucky man!"

"I don't need you to tell me that." Benjamin said proudly.

With raised eyebrows, Axel said, "Chill dude. I love the one I'm with."

Walking back over to Sierra, Benjamin looked back at Axel and said, "Um...I think I just heard someone page your walkie, bro. You might want to get a move on."

"I hear you. Take care, man." Glancing back, he said, "Maybe we can get together sometime. You can meet my lovely wife and kids." Axel sounded excited.

"We'll see, bro, Benjamin said.

Grandma Flo came out to update everyone that Mr. David was fine and that he needed a heart stent put in due to coronary heart disease. She began to thank God for sparing him as tears of joy flooded her face. Carol and James hugged her.

"I'm going to stay with David tonight. They're prepping for surgery, and he'll come home in a couple of days. We've decided to get married at my house in the backyard; nothing fancy."

Seemingly confused, all eyes stared at her.

"Grandma Flo, what's the hurry?" Sierra asked.

"Well, we ain't gettin' no younger, Sierra, and we don't want to play housemates. We want to be married."

Benjamin was stumped. "What's a housemate, Ms. Flo?"

"Shackers, Benjamin! You shouldn't live in the same house with your mate until you're married. The Lord don't like shackin' up. So, David and I are getting married when he gets home from the hospital. I think this is God's way of speeding things up. We've gotta stop taking each other for granted. Life is short and things happen so fast. Besides, it's time for him to retire from all this."

Tasha quietly spoke, "Well, I can stay with Ray-Ray while you guys have the ceremony if you don't mind."

"Thank you so much, Tasha," Carol said. "We would appreciate it. I'm sure Raymond would be grateful as well."

Awaiting an agreeable response from Raymond, everybody looked around. But he wasn't in the room.

CHAPTER 7

SELF-REFLECTION

"Where did I go wrong? How did I allow myself to get here?"

Rayna began to cry and thought about her sacrifice for love—to be loved. The signs she ignored; the red flags that waved before her eyes. Always telling me where to sit; how to sit; what to and not to wear; literally jerking me around.

I remembered when I found out I was pregnant before going to the Bahamas. Several times I thought about telling Elliot. But couldn't because he was acting irately. Then things just turned even crazier.

"Hi, Rayna, I'm Nurse Myers. How are you feeling?"

"Is my baby okay?" Rayna was worried.

The nurse ignored her and said, "Dr. Knight wants you to rest now. He will talk to you in the morning. I will get you some morphine to ease your pain."

Rayna drifted into a deep sleep after the medication was given and the nurse left. She felt as though she was sinking deeper and deeper into a large, black hole surrounded by darkness. Elliot was there! She could hear his voice..."I'm gone get you, ho! You ain't never gone be happy."

Still dreaming, she tried to climb out of the hole, but the walls were so wet and slippery. Elliot kept pulling her back in. "Where you think you going, ho! You coming with me!"

The more she tried to climb out; the deeper she sank. It seemed as though her body was tightly bound by a thick, gooey oil-like substance; as if her life was slipping away.

In the distance, she saw an unusual, glowing light that resembled a giant hand. She began to think about "The Lord's Prayer" that Grandma Flo taught her when she was a little girl. She touched the saturated, slick surface and leaped for the giant, warm hand that reached out to her. It pulled her from the dark hole.

Suddenly, she awakened to the radiant sunlight peeping through the wooden blinds in the room. Struggling to breathe, Rayna whispered, "LORD, thank you for saving me."

With tears streaming down her face, "But what about Elliot?" she thought. "He will never let me go!"

CHAPTER 8

BROTHER?

Before the police arrived, Damon quickly placed a mask on his disfigured face. Looking over at the still carcass lying there, he said, "Elliot, I really hate it ended this way, man."

As numerous police cars, a couple of firetrucks, and an ambulance raced down the driveway through the pouring rain, he rushed to pull the mat over the floorboard.

Boom! Boom! Boom! "Police! Open up!"

In a hurry, he opened the door and Detective Whitmore displayed his badge. He motioned for the paramedics who instantaneously began working on Damon's gunshot wound.

Detective Whitmore knelt beside the cadaver and stepped outside and called the Captain to confirm that the suspect was deceased. Once back inside, he took out his notebook, and inquired, "What's your name, sir? What happened here?"

"Damon Simpson. All I know is that I had just got home and a knock came at the door." Sounding nervous, he continued, "I opened it and this fella jumped me. It happened so fast. We struggled and the gun went off a few times."

"What do you mean a few times?"

"I don't know. Two or three, maybe. Like I said, it happened so fast. I didn't know it was him."

Did you know him?" Detective Whitmore inquired.

Looking at the detective, he tearfully said, "Yes. I didn't understand who it was until it was over. Like I said, when I opened the door, he bum-rushed me. I didn't even realize he shot me! Elliot was my brother! Damon cried.

"Brother?!" Detective Whitmore shouted. "And you killed him?"

Afraid now, Damon yelled, "It was self defense! I didn't know it was him! He was my foster brother!"

Detective Whitmore looked at the Officers and the man suspiciously. Looking around the room, he asked, "So, how long have you been living here, Mr. Simpson?"

"About 9 or 10 years. I hadn't seen Elliot til tonight," Damon sounded agitated.

"Calm down. We are just trying to get to the truth."

"Do I need a lawyer? I told you it was self-defense." Damon sat down on the couch in disbelief. He noticed the mat had shifted due to trodden footsteps.

"Look, no one is accusing you of anything. But there is one more question. Where is your car?"

"Excuse me?" Damon is seemingly annoyed with the line of questioning as Detective Whitmore starts pacing.

"You said you had just arrived home before the suspect came knocking at your door. To be clear, were you out walking in this rainy weather, Mr. Simpson? Do you own a vehicle?"

"No, I don't. Are you arresting me?"

"Of course not! Will you come down with us to the station to make a statement and one of our officers will bring you back home? I apologize but, this is part of my job."

"I guess. I mean, I haven't had any trouble in this neck of the woods before."

Detective Whitmore and the officers gather the duffle bag and Elliot's handgun as evidence. The coroner motions that he's gathered all he needs, so they zip Elliot's bloody corpse in the black body bag.

Damon notices that the Officers and Detective Whitmore have smirks on their faces.

"What's up with that?" Damon murmured to himself as sits in the back of one of the police cars.

CHAPTER 9

AN OLD FAMILIAR PLACE

Finally, the rain stopped. Raymond left the hospital on foot as mad as a roaring fire. He kept beating his head with his fists. "I should've waited. Stupid! Why didn't I wait for her?" he kept saying to himself.

Fists clenched. Jawbone tight. Not realizing how far he had walked, Raymond found himself in the old neighborhood he left behind years ago. He looked ahead staring at "JJ's Liquor Store." He started pacing back and forth while his phone kept ringing.

Tasha wanted desperately to speak to him because he hadn't taken his other meds. He wouldn't answer. Raymond, battling with his inner demons, was trying to decide, "Should I go in or walk away and call Tasha?"

He couldn't stop thinking about Carol. How beautiful she looked with her curvy hips and luscious, soft lips. He longed to touch her silky, smooth skin; her shiny, curly locs.

He sat on the bench outside of "JJ''s" and began to think about that day when Carol kicked him out for leaving Ray-Ray home alone. He thought about how he should've fought for their relationship.

From out of nowhere, a woman walks up to him and says, "Well, hello 'Brown sugar'! Lookin' for some fun tonight?"

When Raymond, looked at her, he immediately thought of Carol and took the lady by the hand.

She took him into the store. "Brown Sugar, I need some pick me up. How about some gin and vodka?"

"Sure, Carol." He grinned, hugged her, and kissed her cheek.

"Who's Carol, Brown Sugar? My name is Lacy. People call me 'Lace'."

"C'mon, Carol let's go home." Raymond ignored her.

"For a price, sweetie. I need cash; no check, money order, or credit card."

"I got you, Carol. I always got you!" He quickly went to the ATM in the store and gave her $500.

His phone rang again.

Lacy took it and asked, "Brown Sugar, who is Tasha? I mean, you're calling me Carol, but Tasha is ringing your phone."

She looked at his hand and realized he was married. "Oh, I see how you play it, Brown Sugar. You a playa for real!"

Raymond grabbed her by the waist and shouted, "I said let's go home, now, Carol!"

"Whoa! Slow down playa. No need to rush things. We need to make a quick stop first so you can take the edge off. She kissed him and tossed his phone in the trash.

Raymond followed along like a kid led by a lollipop. Before he knew it, he was at a very 'familiar place.' Raymond, battling with his inner demons, once more, was trying to decide, "Should I go in or walk away?"

When he looked over at Lacy, he thought only of Carol. He wanted to be with her so badly. He felt that Lacy looked so much like her in her younger days. So beautiful, sweet, and innocent.

Oh, how he yearned to make love to Carol. "Tonight is the night. It's my chance." He thought to himself. Lacy took him by the hand and, they both walked into that 'familiar place' and went back to Lacy's apartment down the street.

CHAPTER 10

WORDS OF WISDOM

Hours later in recovery, David thought of his close call with the grim reaper. As soon as she returned from the bathroom, he said, "Flo! I love you. Marry me, Flo!"

"David, sweetie, you talking outta your head. You need to get some rest. We can talk about it tomorrow."

"Flo, I mean it. Tomorrow is not promised. Get the chaplain up here." He protested.

"Alright," she saw the seriousness on his face and complied.

Carol was lying in James' arms when she rushed over, "Carol! James! David wants to marry me right now!"

"But he just had surgery. Is he sure?" Carol asked.

James turned to Carol and smiled, "Sweetheart, a man knows when he's found his "good thang." He stood to stretch. "You go, David!"

"Yeah, he wants me to get the chaplain right now. I guess you two will have to be the witnesses. How's Ray-Ray?"

"We're going in to talk to her in the morning. The nurse said she was resting." Then, Carol held Flo's hands, "Mama, why don't you just wait. Y'all ain't even got no rings!"

"Um...that's a good point. I'll be right back." She turned to go down the hallway to go talk to David when she heard arguing outside Rayna's hospital room door.

Benjamin and Sierra!

She quickly walked over to them and said without questioning their argument, "Look, listen, and learn you two. There is too much going on in this family right now for petty arguments. It's not about who said or did what. Sit down and talk about what you're feeling and thinking. Spend less time arguing and more time getting to know each other. Your thoughts, likes, dislikes, needs, and wants. Accept that you both have flaws; neither of you is perfect which is why God should be first in your lives so that He can lead and guide. I love you both. Now, I gotta get the chaplain because David and I are getting married tonight!"

They looked at one another dazed and confused.

"Wait!" Sierra snapped back to reality. "Grandma Flo, did you say you and Mr. David are getting married tonight?"

"Well, he said now's the time but, I need to find out about the rings first." She scurried back to his room.

Each thinking about what Grandma Flo said, Benjamin and Sierra apologized to each other and sat near Rayna's door in silence.

When Grandma Flo walked into David's room, he was making paper rings from one of his dietary menus. "Honey, these will have to do until I get outta here. It's what's in the heart that matters anyway; not the ring. That's just a symbol. Now, did you find the chaplain?"

"Going, dear!" As quickly as she entered the room, she left again.

She ran into James and Carol. "Well, he already got the rings!" she said with laughter.

"Where did he get them from, Mama?" Carol and James looked at each other baffled.

"You'll see! C'mon now. Let's find the chaplain!"

CHAPTER 11

DAMON RECOLLECTS

G rateful the rain had stopped, Damon was glad to be home from the station. Detective Whitmore told him he was free to go and thanked him for his cooperation.

Damon remembered that during the interrogation, an officer left the door open to go get him a soda. He overheard a couple of officers talking.

Officer Johnson said, "I'm sure glad that guy nailed him."

"Yeah, that poor girl suffered a lot. I hope she's going to be okay. Officer Young said she lost the baby," Officer Lynch said.

Damon turned on the television and questions were whizzing like racecars at a dragstrip. The Captain kept waving his arms for reporters to calm down so that he and his staff could answer them one at a time. Then, Detective Whitmore took to the podium to talk about the details of the shooting.

"Yes, the suspect, Elliot Nolan, was shot and killed in self-defense while trying to break into someone's home. We have notified his Uncle, Pastor James Nolan who's his only living relative. Biological relative."

The sound of the press conference was quickly fading away from his ears as he began to recollect how he came to know Elliot...

That morning a knock came at the door and Damon's mom opened up. There stood an older black woman with a scrawny African-American teenager who looked about 14 or 15 years old. He acted as though he had a chip on his shoulder.

"Laura, thank you for taking him in so unexpectedly. Elliot's family said he couldn't stay with them anymore, so here he is. I feel you and Damon are the best fit for him. You're such an awesome single mother and have worked wonders with Damon."

"C'mon in y'all." The salt-and-pepper gray-haired lady looked at Elliot with soft, kind eyes. She gave him a big hug. He felt like crying but held back the tears as he thought of his mother.

"Elliot, come on, let's meet, my son, Damon. He's going to be your foster brother."

She walked Elliot over to meet Damon. They both just stood and looked at each other. Damon felt sorry for him and said, "C'mon bruh, let me show you to your room."

Reluctantly, Elliot went with the older boy who somewhat reminded him of Elijah. Maybe it was because he was the same age as Elijah. On the way to the room, Damon apologized to Elliot about the loss of his family and let him know that he was there for him if he felt like talking.

Elliot just walked away and closed the door. He looked around the room. His heart filled with anger and fear, he fell on the bed and cried silently. Oh, how he missed Elijah so!

When Damon returned downstairs, he overheard the social worker and his Mom in the kitchen talking about Elliot.

"I feel sorry for him, Laura, but he has had a rough go of it. I truly hope he can make it with you and Damon these next 6 years. They're going to go ahead and give him at least a third of his trust to help him get established. He will be able to use the money to go to college, get a car, and a place of his own. His family's lawyer is in charge of his estate and funding. He will get the rest when he turns 21. He will be set for life if he uses his senses."

"Well, Mabel, am I getting any of that money? I mean, I am providing a place, food, and..."

"C'mon, Laura, you'll be paid $3,000 a month until Elliot graduates high school."

"Oh, okay. I'm just saying. I mean, I hate the boy lost his family and all, but we need the money. I want Damon to go to school for a computer programmer. He wants to work for that big tech company in Sumnerfield. My boy got computer skills." she said proudly.

"I know. I'm so proud of him, Laura. Has he been stealing lately?" Mabel sounded concerned.

"No, I think he learned his lesson last year once I let him sit in jail for a few hours."

Damon's jawbone tightened as he thought to himself, "You the reason I was stealing. Acting like you didn't tell me to get you one of them fur coats. That's alright cause as soon as Elliot get that money, I'm gone get me a chunk of it! Cha-ching!"

Suddenly, Damon's reminiscence was interrupted by a phone call...

He looked at his phone with a smile from Earth to Heaven and said, "Lord, Lacy, am I glad to hear from you!"

CHAPTER 12

RAYNA AWAKES!

"Elliot! Elliot!" Rayna woke up screaming and crying, "Elliot's dead? I had a dream that Elliot died!"

Tasha held her to comfort her and switched on the television. "Breaking news!" the reporter said, "Suspect, Elliot Nolan, was shot and killed during a home invasion. The police believe the suspect's death was self-defense as the homeowner shot the suspect during a struggle. There will be a police conference at 2:00 this afternoon with further details." Tasha switched it back off.

"Worthless sap! He caused me to lose the baby, Tasha!"

Tasha began to cry and said, "Oh, Rayna, I'm so sorry for all you've been through."

Ray-Ray looked around the room and noticed none of the family was there. "Where is Daddy and Mama? Where's everybody?"

"I'm sorry, but they'll be here later. I'm supposed to keep you company until they arrive. They have so much to talk to you about."

Ray-Ray saw Tasha's solemn face as she quickly looked away. "What's wrong, Tasha? What's going on? There's something you're not telling me."

Tasha began to quiver and cry uncontrollably.

"What is it, Tasha!?," Rayna said in frustration.

BOOM! BOOM! A knock at the door and in walked Dr. Knight, Sierra, and Benjamin.

Sierra and Benjamin rushed over to hug her. Sierra left tears of joy on Ray-Ray's cheek and pillow. "What's going on, Sierra?"

Dr. Knight interjected. "Sierra. Let me tell her, please." Sierra saw that Tasha was crying and went over to console her. Dr. Knight took a deep breath and calmly said, "Rayna, I'm sorry, but you lost the baby."

"I know that! I had a dream and..."

"I'm not finished, Rayna," Dr. Knight continued. "I need you to know that Elliot can't hurt you anymore. He's dead. He was shot and killed while trying to break into someone's home."

"I know that, too! I had a dream and, I just saw it on the news!"

They noticed the television was off.

Tasha replied, "I just cut it off a few seconds ago."

Benjamin turned on the television again. The reporter was interviewing Detective Whitmore who was talking about Elliot's demise and how it transpired. He never mentioned the homeowner's name. Weird. Everyone thought.

The nurse came in to check Ray-Ray's vital signs. Dr. Knight warned that she needed to rest now and recommended everyone come back within a few hours.

Benjamin turned off the T.V. once more. They all hugged her and left the room as Ray-Ray began to drift off to sleep again from the sedative the nurse gave her.

CHAPTER 13

WANDERING SOUL

Raymond awakened with a terrible headache. Feeling groggy and staggering around the room, he tripped over a trashcan and out of it fell a couple of syringes and tissues. He ran to the bathroom and looked in the mirror. "What's going on? How'd I get here?" He looked at his arms. There appeared those familiar marks. He started fumbling through his pockets searching for his phone. He quickly checked his wallet. His credit card was missing; no money. All gone! He only had his driver's license. Out of anger and frustration, he punched the mirror with both fists gashing his knuckles.

Lacy came rushing in. "Fool, what's the matter with you? You done broke my man's mirror! You betta get outta here before he gets back!"

"Who are you? What am I doing here?" Raymond is crying now. "Where's my wife?"

"Which one? First, you called me 'Carol', and then you called me, 'Tasha.' Man, you got some serious issues."

Enraged with fear and madness, Raymond grabbed Lacy by the neck; squeezing tightly, "Where's my phone, ho?"

"You betta get yo' hands off of me!" Lacy yelled. She kicked Raymond where the sun don't shine and ran out of the bathroom!

"Hello? Lacy, are you alright?" The voice on the phone shouted.

Gasping for air, Lacy said, "Yeah, some fool tried to strangle me! You got my money, Damon?"

"Yeah, I got it! Don't forget to hook me up with the Doctor. When do you think he can fix my face?"

"I'll let you know tomorrow, and then we can set up a time and place to get my money. Hey, I have to go. Monty will be back soon and, I gotta get this guy outta here!"

She hung up the phone and with one blow, struck Raymond in the head with a cast iron pan. His limp body fell to the floor. She dragged him outside across the road and called the police. "Hey! It looks like there's a man in a ditch across from my street. He just laying there."

Blood was streaming down Raymond's face when he finally came to. He was sweating profusely and couldn't remember where he was. His head and body ached terribly. He heard sirens coming and panicked. His mind urged him to get up, but his body wouldn't budge. He passed out again.

Officer Young and his partner were the first responders to the call about a body lying near the road. He called for an ambulance and looked for the man's identification. "Raymond Anthony Brown?' The man looked familiar to Officer Young, but he couldn't remember where he had seen him before. He shrugged it off and wondered how the man wound up by the road known as "Drug Avenue."

When the ambulance arrived, the paramedics put smelling salt near Raymond's nose. Dazed and confused, he looked up at the lady and said, "Ray-Ray?" Shaking uncontrollably, he started puking everywhere.

Lacy watched from her window and hoping they would be gone before "crazy" get home!

They rushed him to the hospital with Officer Young and his partner in tow. Sirens blaring.

CHAPTER 14

CHECKING IN

Benjamin and Sierra were leaving the room after David and Flo's ceremony. Hand in hand; reflecting on Grandma Flo's 'words of wisdom.'

Both were upset because Benjamin felt that Axel was flirting with her.

"Listen, Benji, there's no need to be insecure. You are an amazing man...and lover," she added with a smile. "I love you and want to spend my life with you. But I..."

He quickly interrupted, "I love you, too, sweetie. I'm sorry for getting upset and being a little jealous. That doesn't mean I'm insecure!"

He seemed ashamed and disappointed in himself for allowing Sierra to see that side of him.

Looking away from her, his eyes swelled with tears. Sierra turned his face to hers and kissed him gently and ever so tenderly to reassure him of her love.

"Wanna get something to eat?" Benjamin asked shyly.

"Well, I would like us to check on Rayna first. If you don't mind."

"Yes, my Queen!" and he bowed before her. They both were laughing by the time they got to Ray-Ray's room.

Tasha was sitting outside the door. She told them that Ray-Ray was probably still sleeping from the sedative they had given her. She looked visibly tired and upset from crying.

Sierra hugged her and asked, "Still can't get a hold of Raymond, huh?"

"No. But when I do, he's gonna know that I'm tired of his mess. I think it's over, Sierra! Tasha began to cry as Sierra consoled her. Benjamin looked on in sorrow for Tasha and motioned to Sierra that he was going to check on Ray-Ray.

As he entered the room, Rayna was crying as she watched the breaking news again on television about Elliot's death. Benjamin took the remote and turned the T.V. off. "You shouldn't watch this, sis." he sounded concerned about her welfare.

Sierra overheard as she entered the room, "He's right, Ray-Ray."

Benjamin's head turned very swiftly like an owl. "Is Tasha okay, babe?"

"Yeah, she's gonna hang out for a few more hours and head back home tonight. She wants to check on Aunt Hilda Mae and the kids.

Benjamin looked confused. "She ain't gone wait for...?"

Sierra looked at him sharply and hugged Ray-Ray tightly.

"Can you believe it, Sierra? Elliot's gone! I lost the baby, and now I'm not able to do anything to that creep. Even in death, he cheated me. No! I'm mad as _____. And she burst into tears and screams.

Benjamin motioned to Sierra that he'd wait in the hallway. He felt it was too much grief.

Ray-Ray asked, "Where's Tasha and Daddy? Where's everybody?"

Sierra knew it wasn't wise to answer directly so as not to upset or worry Ray-Ray any further.

"Ray-Ray, let's talk to Dr. Knight about getting you in a wheelchair so you can get out of this room. I think a change of scenery will do you good. I'll be back."

She stepped into the hallway to ask Benjamin if he would pick up some food for the three of them because she wanted to get Ray-Ray out of the room for a bit. Reluctantly, he complied. He really wanted to spend quality time with Sierra—to address the argument they had previously.

Looking around for Tasha, Sierra became worried when she no longer saw her waiting in the hallway.

CHAPTER 15

A SURPRISE WITNESS

Tired from the day, Damon lay across the bed. He couldn't sleep, so he rolled on his back and began to reminisce about how Elliot was always sneaking off and getting him to lie for him.

There was one particular day that he decided to follow Elliot. They wound up at someone's house where a lady was staggering around the pool with a bottle of vodka in her hand.

She was on the phone crying and telling someone that she found out her husband fathered a child and didn't tell her about it.

"I'm leaving him!" she shouted. "I don't care if I am the First Lady of the church. He is supposed to be a Pastor!" Then she tossed the finished bottle into the pool.

When she turned around, Elliot was standing in front of her. She looked as though she saw a ghost! Very frightened, she dropped her phone and staggered away from him. She hit her head on the pool rail and fell in.

Struggling against the water, she began to sink. Reaching out for Elliot, she gasped for air.

"Help me, Elliot! Please, help me!" she shouted.

But he just stood there and yelled at her, "Didn't I tell you that you would have your part in my lake?" And just like that, he held her head underwater as she drowned. He glared at her limp corpse with an eerie smile.

Frightened and unprepared for what transpired, Damon peed on himself. Paralyzed by fear. He saw Elliot looking around to make sure no one saw him.

When Elliot finally left, Damon went home, locked himself in his room, took a shower, and went to bed. He was sore afraid to contact the police; after all, Elliot was his brother—foster brother.

Damon got up the next day to eat breakfast and, Elliot was in the kitchen. Laura had left to go grocery shopping.

Elliot noticed that Damon was acting nervous.

"What's wrong with you, man?" Elliot sounding suspicious and walking near him, "You didn't come down for dinner last night."

"Nothin' man. I wasn't hungry." Damon grabbed some strawberry pop tarts and milk and headed back upstairs. He closed his door locking it behind him.

Footsteps trotted upstairs minutes later. Elliot tried opening Damon's door. He became frustrated and said, "What's going on with you, bruh? Open up!"

Afraid to open the door, Damon looked around his room for anything that resembled a weapon that he could strike Elliot with in case he tried to hurt him.

He remembered his aluminum bat that he kept under his bed. Slowly, he opened the door. "What do you want, Elliot?"

"Why are you acting all weird, bruh?"

Reluctantly, Damon sighed and let go of the door while still holding his bat in his hand, "I saw what you did to that poor woman, Elliot. I followed you yesterday because I was curious about where you keep sneaking off to."

Quite shocked, Elliot started pacing back and forth. "So what are you gonna do? Tell the cops or your Mom, snitch!"

Suddenly, Damon saw he had an advantage. He remembered that Elliot was coming into some money soon.

"Well, if the price is right, there won't be anything to tell. You get what I'm saying, bruh?"

"What are you talking about?"

Damon tapped the bat on his bed, "I mean, you are gettin' a lump sum of money soon, right?"

Puzzled and annoyed, Elliot looked at him and said, "How do you know about that?"

"Look, I'm trying to get outta here. I'm tired of being under Mom's thumb. I need at least $25,000 to get me started. in Charlestown."

Pacing back and forth, Elliot finally said, "I'll give it to you but you betta stay outta my way if you know what's good for you."

Damon knew that Elliot meant it and breathed a sigh of relief when Elliot left the room. Out of precaution, Damon locked his door back until his Mom returned.

CHAPTER 16

AMNESIA OR DELUSIONAL?

The ambulance arrived at the hospital seemingly on two wheels like the "Dukes of Hazzard" car. Paramedics were rushing by with Raymond on a gurney as Tasha walked by. She looked over at the man who was hooked up to IV's with an oxygen mask. Despite all that, the man's face looked familiar.

She cried nervously, "Raymond?!"

Blood was oozing down his face. He was unconscious and sweating profusely. Officer Young and his partner came in abruptly and Tasha stopped them to ask, "Officers, what's going on? This man is my husband."

Then, it clicked! Officer Young remembered seeing the man earlier at the hospital. It occurred to him that this was Rayna's Dad! He looked into the disheartening eyes of the man's wife. He didn't have the heart to tell her where Raymond was picked up from.

"Uh, ma'am. I'm sorry, but we don't have much information to go on right now. He was lying by the road, nearly bludgeoned to death. I want to get a statement from him when he's conscious and in a position to talk."

"Where'd you find him?" Tasha asked.

Officer Young tried to find the adequate words to put it nicely to her. He looked at his partner who shrugged his shoulders.

"Well, he was found on the east side of town which is kinda a rough neighborhood."

Forgetting about Raymond's condition and mental instability, anger takes control of Tasha's love for him.

"In other words, y'all found him on a "drug street," right?"

Again, Officer Young looked at his partner who only shrugged his shoulders once more.

Hesitantly, he answered, "Um, yes. Did Raymond have a drug issue before ma'am?"

"Yes! He was doing so well til now," she said sorely.

Officer Young turned as he heard a familiar voice walking through.

"You here again, man?" Benjamin said.

"Yeah, we just found Rayna's Dad by the road. He was beaten pretty badly."

"What? Where at?" Benjamin walked over to Tasha and hugged her.

"What's going on?" Sierra joined the conversation.

"Babe, they just found Raymond beaten up and lying by the road."

"Oh no! Tasha, are you okay? I'm so sorry," said Sierra giving her a hug.

A doctor came out to give an update on Raymond's condition. Letting them all know that Raymond would be fine after a few days in the hospital. They had pumped the drugs from his system and stopped the bleeding. He warned that Raymond had a concussion, and would take some time to heal.

"Is one of you, Carol? He keeps asking for his wife."

CHAPTER 17

PLASTIC SURGERY

It's amazing how unexpected circumstances tend to reinvent the wheel of life. Today, Damon was getting ready to reclaim his life—plastic surgery!

Lacy called him the next morning and told him to meet her at the "Broken Mug Cafe" around 11:00. She reminded him to bring her $5,000 for setting up the meeting between him and the "No-Named" plastic surgeon.

Damon was ecstatic when he got off the phone with Lacy. He strolled over to the mirror and took his facemask off. Rubbing his burned, shriveled, wrinkly face and neck with his equally burned hands, he imagined how he would look once the procedure was completed.

"Plastic surgery is going to work wonders! I can finally be me again."

Damon reminded himself of that horrific day when he followed Elliot...for the second time!

It was hot and sunny...seemed like 100 degrees. Elliot was restless the night before. I could hear him pacing in his room repeatedly murmuring, "They all will have their part in my lake! The lake of fire! And they shall burn well!"

I didn't understand what he meant until I followed him that day to a beautiful two-story, white vinyl-sided house with black shutters and a two-car garage. The house was enclosed with a black iron privacy fence.

As Elliot approached the house with a six pack of beer, there were two attractive young girls...looked like twins, standing in the driveway. They seemed startled to see him. One of the girls hugged him while the other girl looked on suspiciously.

Elliot and the girls started chitchatting as he offered them some beer. A guy came outside and they shook hands while Elliot passed him one also.

I noticed that Elliot wasn't drinking; just doing a lot of the talking.

After the beers were gone, they invited Elliot inside. Yawning, before going in, both the girls seemed tired all of sudden.

I hopped out of my car and crept to the garage window in time to see their bodies passing out on the floor. Elliot standing over them with a sly grin.

It dawned on me that he must've slipped something in their drinks!

He pulled some gloves, from the back pocket of his tattered black jeans. Running back to his car parked around the corner, he put on a mask and grabbed a gas can and lighter.

Next, he bolted the garage door and blocked all exits.

I quickly scurried behind the bushes hoping he wouldn't see me. I wanted to do dial 9-1-1 but forgot my phone while trying to hurry to follow him.

Overcome by fear as to what was happening before my very eyes, I peed on myself. I couldn't move!

It happened so fast! He poured gasoline outside near the entrance and threw the lit matches on it. Elliot set fire to some rags, busted the window that I just ran away from, and lit the house up! He grinned at the blazing flames that engulfed the house. "The lake of fire!" he screamed; then laughed.

Fear left me as my adrenaline kicked in and my feet ran toward the fire. Elliot got a glimpse of me while fleeing the scene and raised his hand making a gun gesture.

As I entered the smoke-filled room from the back entrance, I tried to grab a blanket to cover the girls burning bodies so that I could pull them out. The young man wasn't moving.

I didn't even realize I was on fire! I heard sirens and passed out.

The next thing I knew, I woke up in a burn center badly burned on my face, hands, and legs. I was in so much pain physically and mentally when I found out the others did not survive. They were siblings!

I didn't get the chance to extort Elliot. I never saw him again until that rainy night when he showed up at my door...about 10 years later.

Well, thanks to the money in that duffle bag. I guess that was my way of gettin' paid.

With this plastic surgery, I won't have to live like a hermit any longer. No more jumping trains from town to town or state to state.

I should have enough to live solid for a few months til I land a job.

CHAPTER 18

TASHA'S PLEA

Carol and James were elated to see Ray-Ray up and moving! She was walking a little faster with the use of the walker.

"I'm not in much pain anymore, Mama!" she said while giving Carol a warm hug. James hugged Rayna, turned the television to SportsCenter, and sat down.

"Would you like to go for a walk, sweetie?" Carol asked Ray-Ray.

"Sure!" Carol held the door open for Ray-Ray to take a stroll down the hall. Surprisingly, they both ran into Tasha, Benjamin, and Sierra.

"Hi, guys! I'm so glad to see y'all are still here. Has anyone seen Daddy?" Ray-Ray asked with concern.

They each looked at each other and Sierra walked over to embrace Ray-Ray.

"What's going on?" Carol looked worried.

Benjamin said, slowly, "Well, he's in the hospital. Room C126."

Ray-Ray turned to Tasha. "What happened?"

"I'm not sure." She said seemingly annoyed when she glanced at Carol. "Right now he seems to think your Mama is his wife."

Carol glared at Tasha, "Look, I don't know what's going on or what you're insinuating. I have nothing to do with whatever you two got going on. Leave me and James out of it!"

Ray-Ray butted in. "Will someone just tell me what's going on with my Daddy? She grabbed Tasha by the arm; warning her, "Please lay off my Mama. She don't want Daddy like that."

Sierra interrupted and said, "He got beat up and left by the road in some bad neighborhood. They pumped drugs from his stomach and said he got a concussion."

Benjamin stared in disbelief as Sierra chattered on. "He will recover, but it's going to take some time." Sierra then turned to Ray-Ray and said, "I'm sorry, but he believes she's his wife. I think it might it's amnesia due to the concussion."

Carol sounded annoyed and said, "Again, not me and James' problem, nor our fault." "Now, I hope he's going to be alright and y'all can work through this, Tasha. I really mean that. I don't want or have any desire to be with Raymond."

"Well, that's because you have me, sweetheart." James walked up from out of nowhere. "What's going on?"

The doctor walked out and asked, "Who is Tasha? Mr. Brown is asking for you." Tasha didn't speak up. Instead, she started to walk away.

Ray-Ray said angrily, "Are you serious, right now, Tasha? My Daddy just asked for you and you gone abandon him?"

Sierra begged Ray-Ray to be careful not to get her blood pressure up. "I think you should go back to your room, Ray-Ray to calm down and rest."

"Not til I see Daddy!" She turned the walker and went towards Raymond's room.

Tasha walked up to Ray-Ray and gently placed her hand on her shoulder. She pleaded with her.

"Will you let me talk to him alone, please? I will stay with him tonight so you don't have to worry. Get some rest and see him in the morning. Okay?"

Hesitating, she saw the hurt in Tasha's eyes and said, "Alright. I hope y'all can work it out, Tasha. At least for the kids' sake."

Carol and James helped Rayna back to her room while Tasha went in to talk to Raymond.

Benjamin and Sierra left to see David and Grandma Flo.

CHAPTER 19

MEXICO CITY

D amon was excited and nervous at the same time when he met Lacy at the cafe. "Where and when do I meet the doctor, Lacy?"

"Hold on, Damon!" Lacy was brushing some lint off her faux mink coat.

"C'mon, quit stalling. I wanna get going. There's a new life and a lady that I'm dying to meet."

Seeming curious, Lacy asked, "Well, who might that be? Anyone, I know?"

He reaches into his black leather bag and quickly pulls out a brown envelope. Pushing it across the table to Lacy.

A familiar voice speaks up behind him. "Lacy, who this?" He got ready to grab Damon by the neck. "You cheatin' again?"

She jumped up and gave the envelope to the man. "Nah, Monty. I had to make us some fast cash. I'm hookin' this man up with Doctor Fix. He's on his way to Mexico City! Right, Damon?"

"Is that right?" Monty snatched the envelope from Lacy while pushing her aside. Startled by Damon's grotesque appearance, he nearly tripped over the chair near him. "Man, what happened to you?"

Annoyed by his disrespect to Lacy, Damon didn't answer and just glared deeply into Monty's eyes without a blink. Monty quickly realized that he better back off.

"Alright, man. I might do foolish things, but I ain't no fool. C'mon Lacy, let's get outta here. Good luck, brutha."

As they were leaving, Lacy said, "Mexico City...ask for Doctor Fix. Anybody can tell you who he is and where to find him. Good luck, Damon, and thank you."

Monty grabbed her arm forcefully and told her to "shut up!"

On his way to Mexico City, Damon couldn't help but think about Lacy.

Her sleek, phony smile caused him to worry as she left the restaurant. He would check on her later when he returns.

It took Damon a few hours to get to Mexico City by a flight from Charlotte. First class all the way. Once he landed and got to his hotel, he immediately asked for Dr. Fix. He received a $500 answer right away.

A man met him in the lobby of the hotel and placed a blindfold on Damon while proceeding by limo to the location.

Upon arrival, Damon heard a scraggly voice that sounded like a robot...disguised somehow. The men spoke Spanish so he had a difficult time understanding the translation.

The robotic voice spoke English saying, "Bring him in. Did you get the money...$50,000?"

"Si, Señor." The gentleman who blindfolded Damon replied.

The driver and the man helped him up a flight of steps, sat him in a chair, but did not remove the blindfold.

The man with the robotic voice took a look at Damon and said to the nurse, "Strip him, put on this gown, and help him get on the table. I'm going to wash up."

Damon seemed dazed and confused. "Wait! Can you remove the blindfold so I can do it myself!"

"No talking, please. No conversation. Just do as I ask. Did you bring your paperwork?"

"Yes. It's in my bag." The doctor glanced at the bag and left the room.

The nurse slipped off Damon's blindfold after she helped him on the table.

He looked around the room. It was clean...well-kept. The equipment looked practically new. The windows were blackened out with paint. Two steel doors for an entrance and an exit.

In one corner of the room was a small computer center. Another side of the room had a large brown leather couch with a red flannel blanket draped on one arm of it. There was a large microwave in one corner of the countertop alongside a toaster oven. A steel medium-sized fridge was located near a gas stove. No television. No music. Silence.

Suddenly, a door opened and footsteps entered the room. The man with the robotic voice was fully covered; like in a Haz-mat suit. Damon couldn't tell the man's ethnicity or race.

"Your burns are many and very disturbing. This may cost you an extra $25K." The Doctor looked at his nurse and asked her to bring him the black bag that was lying on the couch.

The nurse quickly gave Damon a shot of something and placed an oxygen mask over his face. Before going under, he saw Doctor Fix walk out one of the steel doors with his black bag.

CHAPTER 20

PEACE OUT

Tasha entered the room to find Raymond lying in bed facing the wall. He was sobbing quietly. She walked over to his side and looked into his teary eyes. She recognized that grief-stricken look from before...when she first met him in prison.

"I'm sorry, Tasha, for everything I've put you through. I don't blame you if you choose to get a divorce. I understand. It's just that I was overcome with jealousy towards James and Carol...of how cozy and loving they are together. It feels like they are flaunting themselves in front of my face."

Tasha blurted out. "How am I supposed to compete with your love for Carol, Raymond? You're still in love with the mother of your child! Listen up and hear me good! When we get back to Kelton, we'll be going to counseling or you can pack your stuff and get out! I'm sick of this!"

She was getting ready to walk towards the door when Rayna came in.

"Hey, Daddy!" She hugs him and kisses his forehead. "I'm so glad you're going to be okay."

"Well, baby girl, I don't know," Raymond said mournfully.

"What do you mean? The doctor said you have a concussion but will recover."

She noticed tears streaming down his face as he was staring at Tasha.

Angrily, Rayna turned to Tasha and said, "What's Daddy talking about, Tasha?"

"Well, I told your Daddy I'm tired of his "confusion" about his love for Carol and jealousy of James. Either he goes to counseling when we get home or it's over between us. No disrespect to your Mama, Rayna, but I'm not going to compete with their past."

"Exactly, Tasha! Their past!" Rayna shouted and turned to Raymond, "Right, Daddy?"

Raymond didn't answer right away—just stared blankly and looked up at the ceiling.

"Right, Daddy?" Ray-Ray asked again as if he didn't understand what she said.

He finally looked at her and said, "Tasha's right, Ray-Ray. It's not fair to her. I am confused. I think time apart will do us both some good. I will go to counseling on my own terms...not because of an ultimatum. So, I think I should move in with you for a little while, Ray-Ray until..."

"Wait! What? Now Daddy I don't mean no harm, but that's a "No!" You need to go on back with Tasha and figure this out. Mama ain't coming back to you. What y'all had is over and gone! She truly loves James. Get over it!"

Tasha butted in. "I'm sorry, Ray-Ray, but your Daddy can't stay with me."

Walking toward the door, she looked back at Raymond and replied, "I want a divorce. Your things will be in the guest room at the house waiting for you to pick them up. When or if you decide to come back to Kelton."

Raymond looked at Tasha wild-eyed. "Don't be foolish, girl! I just need time to think!

Tasha rolled her eyes at him and said, "I'm too young to wait and too old for you to figure it out."

"But, what about the kids? They need me." Raymond argued.

"They need both of us, Raymond. And we can't have peace of mind as long as there's confusion between us."

"So you gone desert me in my time of sickness! You know I have a concussion! Through sickness and health, Tasha. For better or worse."

"Are really gone try to throw some vows at me when you sittin' up here committing adultery. Lusting after a woman that ain't yours. Screw you and your concussion!

She hugged Rayna and left.

CHAPTER 21

BENJAMIN'S SURPRISE

That morning, Grandma Flo kept looking at the one-carat diamond ring David had waiting for her in the kitchen at the coffee bar. She placed the "paper-made" ring in the box as a keepsake and reminder of David's love for her.

David admired looking at the silver wedding band Grandma Flo had left for him in the bathroom on the sink that same morning. He placed the "paper-made" ring in the keepsake box to remind him of how he seized the opportunity—a man that "findeth a good wife; findeth a good thing."

"David, are you okay, honey?" Grandma Flo hollered out from the kitchen.

"I sure am baby cakes. Do you mind getting me some coffee, love?"

"Of course not!" She smiled from Earth to Heaven. "I was getting ready to make some anyway."

The doorbell rang. Mr. David tried to get up to answer when Grandma Flo came hurrying from the kitchen. "Sit down somewhere! I'll get it. You just relax, sweetheart!"

She peeped out the blind from the living room. "Oh! It's Benjamin and Sierra!" she said happily. "C'mon in lovebirds! How are you?"

After hanging their belongings on the coat rack, she asked Sierra to help her with the coffee.

"Sure! I need a cup anyway. Baby, would you like some 'Joe'?" Sierra said candidly to Benjamin.

"Yeah, I'll take a cup." he said grinning at her from Earth to Heaven.

Mr. David noticed and waited til the ladies were out of sight.

Jokingly, he said, "It looks like I'm not the only one who got snatched by Cupid!"

As laughter rang out from the kitchen, Benjamin pretended to ignore what Mr. David said and kept his eyes glued to the television.

Mr. David repeated amusingly, "Uhm...I said 'it looks like I'm not the only one who got snatched by Cupid', young man!"

Benjamin looked at him a little embarrassed. "Is it that obvious, Mr. David?"

"It certainly is, son. I'm happy for you two. But, do you mind if I give you a piece of advice?"

"Sure!" Benjamin sat up attentively.

"Always express your love to the woman and she will please you well! A King must sacrifice for his Queen! His virtuous woman!" he said wisely.

"Absolutely. Man, I love her so much, Mr. David. I hope I..."

Sierra came running into the room like a puppy-in-love teenager, "Baby, which creamer? Hazelnut or Peppermint

Mocha? I know I'm the sugar, so no need to put that in your coffee." She kissed him gently on the cheek.

"You got that right, my Queen! I'll take your butt...I mean, Hazelnut." Benjamin said laughingly.

Seeing he was distracted now, Mr. David reminded Benjamin of their conversation once Sierra strolled back into the kitchen.

"You were saying, Benjamin?"

"Well, I hope I'm making the right decision to ask her to marry me," he said nervously looking at David. "I mean, when is the right time?"

"Young man, when you got *"that feeling,"* you'll know. *"That feeling"* that makes you feel inseparable. *"That feeling"* when you just want to hold each other all day and night...not saying a word among you. *"That feeling"* that makes you light up every time she enters the room. *"That feeling"* where you are telepathic—you know her thoughts and she knows yours. *"That feeling"* when every moment without her, feels empty. She's the batter in your cake and puts that pep in your step."

Flo came waltzing in with the tray of coffees, and Sierra was not far behind with napkins.

"What y'all in here talking bout?" Flo asked with curiosity.

Sierra joined Benjamin on the couch and was about to pass him his cup of coffee when suddenly he stood up. Then got down on one knee in front of her. He looked into Sierra's big, beautiful brown eyes and gently cupped her left hand saying, "Sierra, my love! You are the batter in my cake. And it is you that puts the pep in my step. I love you, baby. Will you do me the honor of becoming my wife?"

Mr. David smiled and said, "I know you didn't. Imma let you have that young man. Congratulations!" He and Florence cheered.

Sierra began to cry, grabbed her coat, and ran outside.

CHAPTER 22

SECOND CHANCE

Damon felt woozy coming out from under the anesthesia when he heard, "Nurse! Bring me those scissors, please."

He still could not recognize the Doctor's face because he was fully covered except his eyes.

She scurried over to hand them to "Doctor Fix" who carefully started clipping the bandages from Damon's face. Overcome with intense excitement and nervousness, Damon began to flinch.

"Calm down, sir. I understand your elation, but you have to remain still, Damon. It looks like everything turned out fine, except there is one burn mark I couldn't seem to repair very well. The one on your left knee. It appears it's a lifetime scar. Nonetheless, your face and everywhere else look great! You'll be here another week or so to completely heal, and then you can get on with your new life, young man!"

After unwrapping all the bandages from Damon's face and body, "Doctor Fix" told the nurse to bring a mirror. Before getting a glimpse of himself, "Doctor Fix" reminded Damon to remain calm.

Anxiously, Damon took the handheld mirror and raised it to his face. He was overcome with joy and began to cry.

His skin was pecan brown and smooth...handsome as can be!

"I can't believe it! It's really me...I look like me again! Oh my God! Thank you, Lord!"

Suddenly, he fell to his knees. He didn't look like a monster anymore!

The nurse was staring at Damon in disbelief and admiration. She had seen "Dr. Fix's" work before but this was phenomenal. No wonder he gets paid the big bucks.

She said, "You're a walking miracle, Damon! I hope everything works out for you in the States. If not, you can certainly come..."

"Uhm...uhm," Dr. Fix jealously interrupted, "This man has bigger fish to fry so move along, minnow and get him some water and clothes, please."

She rolled her eyes at him and walked off like a spoiled brat.

Dr. Fix disregarded her tantrum and asked, "So, Damon, what are you going to do when you get back home?"

He thought about his Mom...how much he missed her. She had passed, and he hadn't visited her grave in quite a while. He longed to talk to her.

"I think I'll visit my Mom before I..." Then he stopped abruptly.

"Before what?" Dr. Fix asked curiously and stared at him.

Damon looked away and glared at the floor as though he were looking for a contact lens.

"Oh, I get it. A young lady, right?"

"Why do you say that?" Damon sounded startled as he was getting dressed.

"Your eyes said it all," answered Dr. Fix. "Who is the lucky one? If you don't mind my asking."

Carefully, putting on his socks, Damon hesitated then saw no reason not to tell him. He looked at "Dr. Fix" and said, "I will tell you only if you tell me your real name."

"Well, I don't need to know that bad. Forget I asked."

Then, he gripped Damon's hand firmly and said, "It's "Dr. Fix" and that's all you need to know."

Damon looked into "Dr. Fix's" eyes. They seemed cold and frightening. He knew the man was serious and snatched his hand from Dr. Fix's grasp.

"Okay, Doc. I get it. We'll both just keep our secrets to ourselves. How bout that?"

Dr. Fix" motioned for him to check himself out in the full-length mirror.

Damon walked over and stared at himself in the looking glass with amazement. He pointed to the fine hunk in the mirror and said, "It's good to be me again!

Time to exercise and get in shape! Thank you, Lord, for a second chance!"

CHAPTER 23

FINALLY, RELEASED

After Tasha left the hospital Kelton-bound, Ray-Ray gawked at her Dad in shock that he would just give up his marriage for false hope.

"Daddy, you're crazy for letting Tasha go like that. You're willing to give up her and the twins! For what?"

"I'll win your Mama back, Ray-Ray. You'll see. I can't help how I truly feel. I think this is fate."

"Nah, Daddy, this is foolish! I suggest you stay away from Mama and James. You're not only hurting yourself but everyone else around you. You need God, some serious therapy, and medication!"

"Nah, baby girl, I only need your Mama."

"No offense, Daddy, but Mama needs her *"peace of mind;"* not *"half of a man."* Leave her alone! I'm warning you!"

"Now wait a minute, Ray-Ray. Who you think you talking to like that? I'm your Father! Have respect."

Ray-Ray snapped back, "Respect? Says the one who is trying to destroy his own marriage and someone else's! You sittin' up here bein' a hypocrite.

"Ain't gone tell you no more! I'll leave you outta the will!" he threatened.

Ray-Ray began to cry. "Losing your money means nothing to me but, if you try to come between Mama and James, you will lose this daughter!"

She stormed out of the room.

When Rayna returned to her room, she sat on her bed and thought of all the crap Elliot put her through; including the loss of her baby.

She buried her face in the pillow and sobbed profusely. The nurse came in to check her vitals and asked if she could get her anything.

Rayna thanked her and politely told her "no."

Suddenly, Dr. Knight came in.

"Well, young lady, you're free to go home today. I am prescribing some pain meds, and you need to follow up with your primary doctor within a few days."

He saw that Rayna was crying. He touched her shoulder to console her. "You all right?"

Rayna looked down at the floor. "Sure, Dr. Knight. I will call my doctor tomorrow."

I don't feel you should stay home alone tonight. Why not..."

Carol and James walked into the room as he was talking. "What's going on, Ray-Ray?" Carol asked.

"I'm being released today, and he doesn't think I should stay home alone tonight."

James quickly chimed in, "I agree. You will stay with us tonight and as long as you need til you feel better."

Ray-Ray walked over and gave James and Carol a hug. "I love you guys."

She turned to James and said, "I am so glad Mama met you. I feel you really saved her life."

Carol and James looked at each other and smiled.

Dr. Knight said, "Um, folks you can take her home now. Please make sure she follows up with her primary doctor within the next few days. I'll go get her paperwork."

"Thank you, Doctor," Carol hugged him and James shook Dr. Knight's hand.

She turned to Ray-Ray and asked, "What's going on? Are you all right?"

No, Mama. It's Daddy. I think he's off the deep end. He's leaving Tasha because he thinks you're coming back to him. I told him that you've already had a piece of a man...twice and that James has brought peace into your life."

James started pacing back and forth. "No disrespect, Carol, but I'm not going to stand by and let this happen. I will talk with him. Man-to-man, okay?"

"Okay, baby." She walked over and kissed him. "I love you, James."

Dr. Knight came in with the papers and said his goodbyes. Rayna grabbed them both by the hand and said, "Let's go guys."

CHAPTER 24

INTERESTING ENCOUNTER

Back in Kelton now, Tasha realized her car was nearly out of gas and wouldn't make it home. She used her sleeves to wipe away the tears from her puffy eyes as she pulled up to "Happy Jack's Gas & Grocery."

On her way into the store, an average-height, dark, handsome, muscular-built gentleman bumped into her abruptly. She fell to the pavement in disbelief and anger. "Watch it, fool!" She shouted at him.

When she tried to get up. Her left shoulder and arm were in excruciating pain.

"I'm so sorry, ma'am!" He stooped down to help her up. She was wincing in pain.

"I'm a Doctor. Can I take a look at your shoulder and arm, please?"

Tasha looked into his soft, kind-hearted brown eyes. Her pain didn't seem as agonizing anymore. As he helped her to her feet with his hand wrapped around her waist, she fainted into his arms.

When she came to, she was lying on a church pew that imitated a park bench outside the store. The gentleman was kneeling beside her.

"Are you okay? Can you hear me?" he politely questioned her.

Suddenly, she sat up, and replied, groggily, "I...I can hear you." Trying to move her left arm, she cried out, "Oh, Lord have mercy! My arm! It hurts so badly. I believe it's broken!"

"Should I call an ambulance or your husband? Uh, Mrs.?"

"Go on head and call an ambulance cause I ain't got much of a husband. She tried to prop her arm. "Oh...what's your name?"

Staring into those lovely, big round brown puffy eyes, he couldn't resist. "Dr...um...Saunders. Dr. John Saunders. And your name, Mrs.?"

Still grimacing in pain she tried to smile. "Nurse Hocutt. I mean, Brown. Tasha Brown." She felt so embarrassed. She couldn't believe she had given him her maiden name.

The store clerk ran over and said he phoned for an ambulance to come to the store.

"Thank you!" They both said in unison sounding relieved.

"Okay, Nurse Hocutt, Brown, uh...Tasha," he said with laughter, "Do you mind if we exchange phone numbers so that I can check up on you later?"

"Well, that's just creepy. And besides, I don't think your wife would approve of you calling to "check-up" on a non-patient." she said.

Smiling from Earth to Heaven, he answered, "Well, if you must know, gorgeous, I haven't found a good one yet; therefore, I remain single at the moment.

Flirtingly, Tasha said, "Probably cause a fine brutha, like you, ain't nothin' but a playa."

"Okay. What about you? Shouldn't I be calling your husband to let him know what's going on? I'm pretty sure he may be worried where you are. I certainly would be."

She bitterly replied, "I'm pretty sure he ain't. We've recently separated." Tasha was still upset with Raymond.

"I'm sorry to hear that," Dr. Saunders said licking his lips as the ambulance arrived.

Tasha blushed and batted her eyelashes like a teenager.

Before the paramedics closed the door, he smiled at Tasha and said, "You know what, here is my number. Let me know how much the bill is, and I will take care of it. After all, beautiful, it was my fault."

"Whatever! Don't hold your breath."

She took the number and dropped it in her purse.

CHAPTER 25

SIERRA'S FEAR

B enjamin was devastated and embarrassed as he saw the confusion on Mr. David and Grandma Flo's faces. He felt frozen stiff. He couldn't believe what just happened.

"Young man, stop standing there and go after her," Mr. David demanded.

"What for?" Benjamin shouted. "So she can cut my throat too. She's already stabbed my heart!"

He sat down on the couch, put the ring back in the box, and tossed it on the coffee table.

Grandma Flo sat next to him and put her arm around him as he began to cry.

Mr. David looked out the window and spotted Sierra sitting on the steps with her face in her hands. Sobbing.

They convinced Benjamin to go outside and talk to her.

He grabbed his coat, went outside, and sat next to her. "What's up, Sierra? Don't you love me?"

Sierra lifted her head and held him so tight, "Of course, you know I do, Benji. It's just that I have seen so many failed marriages throughout my lifetime. In my family, on my job, and even in the church. What if you wake up one day and decide I'm not good enough for you?"

Benjamin looked deeply into her eyes and started wiping away her tears. "Sierra, I love you with all my heart, baby. I ain't trying to let you go. Now, if you feel we need to wait, then we can do that. Just please don't leave me."

"Listen, all I'm saying is that marriage is one of the biggest investments we will make in our lifetime. I mean, Benji, we're talking about growing old together—til death do us part. I can't bear the thought of you not wanting me anymore and leaving me for some young heifer."

He grabbed her by the hands and pulled her close to him. She could feel his heart beating like a drum. Oh, how safe she felt in his arms!

She nestled her head further into his sculpted, muscular chest. They both felt warm inside and out; no longer feeling the harsh blowing wind or cold against their intertwined bodies.

She looked up and kissed him gently on his nose and asked, "Benjamin Robert Murphy? May you please do me the honor of becoming my husband?"

Benjamin cried and whisked her around as she tightly held on; giggling like a schoolgirl. "You better know it!" he shouted.

They rushed inside to tell Grandma Flo and Mr. David who were spectating like two little chatty birds through the window.

CHAPTER 26

WHAT'S GOING ON?

Damon tossed his keys and backpack on the granite-top kitchen island and got a cold brew from the fridge. He turned on the television to CNN to listen to the top stories of the day.

One reporter stated: "The FBI's sources are certain that "incognito" is back in or near Kelton, NC. His real name is Joseph Pembroke, and he is a person of interest in several 'missing persons' cases. If you see this man, then contact your local authorities. Do not try to apprehend or approach him on your own. He is believed to be armed and dangerous."

Damon glanced at the photo and shattered glass splattered onto the floor. He couldn't believe the face he was staring at on the screen! Nearly tripping over the spillage for trying to get a closer look, he yelled, "No way! That looks like Monty!"

All of sudden, Damon was frightened for Lacy. He remembered how angry Monty behaved because he suspected she was cheating on him!

Damon thought. "Oh no!" He quickly got dressed and said, "I have to find Lacy! I need to make sure she's alright!"

Rushing over to her place, he was hoping not to run into him. Knocking on the door, he heard a faint creaking noise as it crept open.

"Lacy!" he shouted. But there was no answer. The house was in disarray. Dishes broken; clothes scattered.

Damon jumped when his phone rang. "Lacy! Where are you?"

Nervous and almost out of breath, Lacy said, "I had to get outta there, Damon. Monty done lost his mind. He done blew the money on gambling and drugs and want me to hustle you for another five grand. Now I got to go somewhere. I got a ticket heading back to my peoples in Louisiana. He dare not come down there. I gotta go now, Damon. You won't be able to reach me at this number no more. I'm tossing this phone and getting a new number. Goodbye, friend. I'm glad we met. You was always nice to me and never judged me. Thank you for that."

And just like that, she hung up. "Wait, Lacy, what..." I tried calling her several times. Nothing.

Damon felt tears streaming down his face and quickly left before Monty showed up. He didn't have the chance to warn her that Monty was on the loose and wanted by the FBI.

Exhausted when he returned home, Damon turned on the television to hear from CNN: "Breaking news, John Pembroke is dead. John Pembroke was shot and killed by two armed security guards while trying to steal a car from the Lyon's Chevrolet car dealership.

He hated Monty died like that but was relieved for Lacy's safety. "I pray she be alright now, Lord."

CHAPTER 27

BROTHERLY LOVE

Hasheem was infuriated that Rakim was breaking his promise with Deana. He swore he would give up his whorish ways to keep their family together.

Growing up, Hasheem and Rakim were always competitive. Each trying to one up the other. Rakim was more handsome, muscular build, but egocentric. While Hasheem was cute, mediocre, and easygoing. When Hasheem talked of being a doctor, Rakim followed suit.

In college, Hasheem regretted telling Rakim how fond he was of Deana Chavis. Naturally, Rakim felt challenged to outshine his older brother...again. As Hasheem thought of Deana; how he lost her to his brother, he became enraged with jealousy...envy. He reflected upon the day when he first met Deana.

Standing in the commons area that crisp, cool autumn morning at Kelton University with her friends laughing and talking, she dropped a book: "Geography Abroad." Casually, Hasheem strolled over to pick it up. He quickly complimented Deana saying, "My beautiful queen, your lovely presence would greatly be appreciated if you would accompany me on a date to "The Crab Shack." And he took her hand in his and gently kissed it. After the "ooh's and ahh's," Deana quickly inclined. She was impressed how emboldened he was to ask her in front of her friends and random strangers.

When Rakim saw them there, he rushed over to introduce himself. He, too, was smitten by Deana's radiant smile and at how gorgeous she was. Those long, lustrous curls, her smooth caramel soft skin, and slim, vivacious body.

Hasheem walked off to get a table for them and asked Rakim to keep an eye on Deana for him. Rakim swooped in like a vulture on a bloody rodent.

"Hey girl, what you want with that nerdy-looking brother of mine? You should be on a date with me. I promise you I can show you a better time." And he leaned in to kiss her on the cheek.

Startled, Deana said shyly, "Well, I think your brother is nice...and cute." She rolled her eyes at him and moved away.

"Yeah, but who wants nice. That's so boring. I'm adventurous...an explorer."

This piqued Deana's interest. "Geography is my major. I'm studying to become a geographer and live abroad. What are you an explorer of?"

Rakim charmingly whispered in her ear, "Come with me and you'll find out. I bet I can discover all your geographic locations!" He tenderly stroked the back of her neck.

Deana blushed. Her body felt hot all over. She liked the charismatic vibe; the touch of his masculine hands. Something about him made her want to know more; feel more. Perhaps that mysterious, daredevil attitude.

She quickly backed away from Rakim when she saw Hasheem approaching.

"I hope my little bro is not boring you. C'mon, I have us a table." Hasheem put his arm around Deana's small waist and gingerly escorted her to the table. Rakim looked on sneakily.

The three of them talked and laughed a lot throughout the dinner. Each brother trying to make sure Deana noticed the best qualities within them. Finally, Hasheem had had enough of Rakim and said, "Hey, bro, aren't you supposed to meet Zara, your girlfriend? To walk her home from work?"

Deana scoffed, "Oh, so you already taken?"

Seemingly annoyed and frustrated with Hasheem, Rakim turned toward Deana and stated, "Don't get it twisted beautiful. I mean, if you can call 6 months with somebody being 'taken.' It's not that serious to me."

Hasheem fired back, "Well, I bet Zara would beg to differ."

"Listen, Hasheem, why you telling her about Zara." he said pushing him.

Pushing Rakim back, he said, "The question is why are you not telling my date about your girlfriend?"

Deana became disappointed about what seemed like high-school bickering and told Hasheem she would talk to him later.

But "Later" never came for Hasheem until she married Rakim.

CHAPTER 28

RAYMOND'S OBSESSION

Finally released from the hospital, Raymond takes an Uber to Ray-Ray's house only to find she's not there. So, he has the driver head over to Grandma Flo's.

Grandma Flo was busy making lunch for David when a loud knock came at the door. "Now who's that knocking on this door like they the police!" Frustrated, she whisked open the door and her mouth dropped. She just stood there staring at Raymond; flabbergasted.

"Sweetie, who is it?" David was eager to know.

"Uh...it's Raymond, honey." Then she sighed, "Raymond, what are you doing here? And where's Tasha?" She glanced over at the Uber driver's car trying to see if she could locate her.

"Florence, please. I'm looking for Ray-Ray. I went by her place and she wasn't there. I need to talk to her."

"Well, she's in Kelton with James and Carol until she's ready to go back home. And you sho' ain't going there bothering them. I'll have Ray-Ray contact you."

Grandma Flo looked at Raymond closely. Something's not right. He seemed fidgety and nervous-acting. "What's going on Raymond? Where is Tasha?"

David, still sitting in the recliner, seemed annoyed that Florence had not invited their guest in yet.

"Florence, sweetie, are you going to invite our guest in or just stand there and interrogate the man to death?"

"Oh, sorry honey. Where are my manners? David's right. Won't you come in, Raymond?"

He quickly shoved his way past Florence and spoke to David. "How are you, sir? Congratulations on the marriage. I'm working on getting mine together too."

"That's awesome, young man. Ain't nothing like settling down with a good woman who always there for you."

"Yeah, you're right. I realize that now. That's why I gotta talk to Ray-Ray."

David suddenly noticed that Raymond was by himself.

"Hey, speaking of a good woman, where's yours?"

Raymond smiled from Earth to Heaven and said, "Don't worry David, I'm going to get her back. Carol, has always been the woman for me. I was too stubborn and dumb to see it earlier."

David rose up from his seated position as if something had bit him on his back. "What do you mean? Raymond, have you lost your mind?"

Florence went over and slapped Raymond's face trying to snap him back into reality. Then David got up and stood between them looking sternly at Raymond to warn him not to touch her. Florence reached around David and pushed Raymond. "Get outta this house, Raymond! And leave Carol and James alone! Go on and find Tasha and make things right with her. I mean it...get outta here, now!"

Florence began to cry and David consoled her. He turned to him and said, "Son, I don't know what's going on with you, but please seek professional help. Go ahead and leave now. You've upset my wife enough."

Remembering that David was an ex cop, Raymond cautiously backed away then ran out the door. The Uber driver, who was watching nosily from a distance, sped off, and left Raymond standing there...his mouth gaped open.

"Oh fudge! I shoulda rode with Tasha had I known Ray-Ray was already in Kelton," he murmured to himself. He looked back and saw David and Florence peering out the window of the open door. As he walked slowly up their driveway, David shook his head and closed the door.

CHAPTER 29

GOOD NEWS

"Hey girl! I got some good news!"

Rayna was still groggy from her medication she had taken earlier that morning while listening to Sierra's euphoric voice on the phone.

"What in the world is going on with you?"

Sierra was exhilarated with excitement. You could tell she was on cloud nine. In that fever-pitched voice she shouted, "Guess who's getting married?"

Ray-Ray couldn't help but joke with her. "Um...let me guess...well, Grandma Flo and Mr. David just got married. Um..."

Sounding annoyed, Sierra said, "Quit playing around Ray-Ray!" You know it's Benji and me!"

Ray-Ray burst out with laughter, "I know, girl. I was just messing with you. I'm really happy for you guys." Then, there was complete awkward silence.

"Ray-Ray, you okay? I'm sorry. I didn't even ask how you were doing. Can I come over to see you?," Sierra said worriedly.

"It's all right girl. You know it's going to take some time to get over the hell that demon put me through. I'm not home though. I'm at mama's...per doctor's recommendation. You're more than welcome to drop by. We'd be glad to see you so that you can spread the good news!"

"Yeah. Benji's telling James today!" Sierra could hardly contain herself with a smile from Earth to Heaven. "We'll be there in a few minutes."

Sierra saw that Benji had beeped in twice during her conversation with Ray-Ray. She felt guilt ridden by the fact that she didn't answer right away.

"I hope he don't be mad when I call him back," she whispered to herself.

"Hey, baby, I got some good news!" Benjamin said right away.

Surprised he wasn't upset, she said, "What is it babe?"

"Sierra, I got us a house! You won't believe where?"

Sierra wanted to be as equally excited instead anxiety choked her heart. She could feel a well of tears overflowing down her cheeks.

Benjamin, puzzled that Sierra didn't give an immediate response, breathed with a deep sigh.

"Babe, are you still there?"

"Benji, what did you do?" She began to cry. "We haven't even discussed buying a house! I don't wanna leave Sumnerfield!"

Benjamin tried to calm her right away and was extremely apologetic.

"I'm sorry, sweetie, for not telling you. I wanted to surprise you. I needed you to see that I can take care of you without involving your finances. Can you meet me at your place, please?"

Sierra was gathering herself when she realized she told Ray-Ray that she would come for a visit.

"Okay, baby." Sierra said reluctantly, "But I just told Ray-Ray I was coming for a visit."

"Perfect! We can go together? I would love to see her too. I just got off the phone with Dad! Did you tell her about us getting married?!"

"Yes." Sierra couldn't help but feel that she had hurt Benjamin's feelings. She thought about how he must truly love her to buy it and not use any of her monies.

Suddenly, she heard him say, "So, my Queen, although you're upset with me right now, you still love me, right?"

"Oh, I love you so much, Benji! Even if it's a shack with one window, dirt floors, and..."

"I love you too, babe," he quickly interrupted. "I'll see you in a few."

When she got home, Sierra wandered around her house to each room. She thought about how she bought the house as a young, single, black female. She worked so hard to get to where she is. Deep inside, she knew she loved Benji with all her heart but wasn't sure about this so-called new house and the move. "I just can't leave Sumnerfield. All my friends are here...my business and ____."

Startled by a knock at the door, she wiped away her tears with the bell-bottom sleeves of her teal green blouse. "Hi, Benji!"

He hugged her tightly and kissed her gently on her neck. Then he looked into her beautiful brown, teary eyes. "What's wrong, baby?"

"My business, Benji. I love you but ____."

"I love you too. No ifs, ands, or buts about it. This is going to work out. You will see. C'mon." He hugged her again, grabbed her by the hand, and walked her to the car.

They drove around town. Everything was looking familiar to Sierra. Driving near Ray-Ray's townhouse slowly, they stopped two houses past hers. There was a sign in front of the house that read: "Sold by Royal Realty Properties."

On the other side of Ray-Ray, a sign read: "For Sale by Royal Realty Properties."

Sierra, with bright, wide eyes, was speechless. She peered at Benjamin and saw how proud and fascinated he was. She realized that he really does care for her and how she feels.

She fell into arms as tears streamed down her face like a flowing river.

Benjamin held on to her and said, "Anything for you, Sierra, is yours. I know how much Ray-Ray means to you...to me...as a sister. She needs us, baby."

CHAPTER 30

NO THREAT; NO WORRIES

"Hey Grandma. I'm fine. What's wrong? You sound upset. Yeah, Mama got her phone. It must be on vibrate." Frantically, Ray-Ray rushed over to Carol and passed her the phone.

Hey, Mama, what's wrong?"

Florence was furious. "If I could, I would cuss right now. But the Holy Spirit won't let me. It's that so-and-so Raymond. He just left here talking about he gone get you back or some craziness like that. I think he done lost his mind, Carol. I was calling to warn you and James because he on his way to Kelton to see Ray-Ray. Says he need to talk to her immediately."

James walked into the living room and saw the distraught look on Carol's face. "Baby, what's the matter?"

Ray-Ray pulled him to the side as Carol continued her conversation with Florence. "James, Daddy done lost his mind. He talking bout he gone win Mama back or some nonsense like that."

"You betta believe it's nonsense!" James shouted. Pounding his fist on the table, he said, "That's all right, when I'm done with him, he gone have all his senses; and possibly an extra one. Ain't nobody interfering with me and mine."

Carol gave Ray-Ray back the phone, grabbed James by the hand, and hugged him. She insisted Raymond was not a threat to their marriage and was only the biological father of her daughter.

A swift knock came at the door. The three of them stopped in dead silence and stared at each other. James' face tightened and he clenched his fist as he reluctantly walked to the door. Flinging it open, he said, "Now looka here...you ___!"

Unexpectedly, Benjamin and Sierra's smiles of joy went to confused frowns while James went from anger to embarrassment. Awkward.

"Well, don't just stand there, James, let them in," yelled Ray-Ray! She pushed past him and grabbed Benjamin and Sierra by the hand to welcome them in.

Sierra looked on in bewilderment. "Girl, what's going on?"

"Girl, Daddy talking bout he gone win Mama back! He on his way here to talk to me about something, Grandma Flo said."

Benjamin seemed a little perturbed. "Would y'all like us to come back another time, Daddy? I mean..."

"Nah, son. Raymond done gone foolish. Supposed to be on his way here."

Benjamin glared at Carol who appeared anxious. He carefully approached her to give her a hug. She flinched.

"I'm sorry, Carol. I didn't mean to frighten you," Benjamin said.

"It's okay, Benjamin. I just..." and she began to cry. "I just want Raymond to leave us alone."

James grabbed her and held her close. "No worries, baby, I got this."

Suddenly, Sierra and Ray-Ray burst out with laughter like they were back in middle school. "Congratulations!" Ray-Ray screamed. They ran over to show James and Carol the engagement ring.

Benjamin motioned to Sierra that it might not be the right time, but she was so overwhelmed with joy and ignored him.

James hugged them both and said, "I'm happy for you guys even though we're not surprised."

Another knock came at the door. As James peered through the blinds, an old pickup truck playing country tunes pulled off.

CHAPTER 31

LETTING GO OF THE PAST

"What am I going to do?" Damon thought to himself as he raced his car down the street toward home. He thought about his friendship with Lacy. How she befriended him without care of his ghastly-looking appearance. Lacy felt more like the sister he never had. There friendship was strictly plutonic and, they could talk to each other about everything.

He remembered telling Lacy about his past life with Elliot. How troubled and sinister Elliot was about getting revenge for the death of his brother, Elijah. Damon also shared details of his childhood as well.

She was so comfortable to conversate with and such a receptive listener.

My mother always struggled with finances due to her impulsive shopping sprees and often living above her means. We always had difficulty making ends meet. My clothes mostly came from consignment stores or yard sales and kids teased me at school. I resented her for that without realizing my mother had a few addictions: lying, gambling, shoplifting, and scam artist. Spending money to gamble instead of paying bills on time. Lights getting cut off, no groceries, and having to go to food banks instead.

When she started taking in foster kids and the money started rolling in, I was so grateful not only for the finances but for having someone around. I watched her scam money...lie, cheat, or steal from the system to get it. I learned from the best.

Mom taught me it was okay to "take" because the system had plenty to "get" and would always receive more. "They won't ever be broke, son, so we can go ahead and get a little now," she'd proudly say with justification.

Damon didn't want to live that type of life anymore. "I've got to do something. I believe this is my second chance to do right. A new life. I don't have to lie, cheat, and steal any more."

Vivid memories of his mother came to his mind. She was gone now...passed away with a heart attack. "Mama, I love you...but you were wrong. And so was I."

He started bawling his eyes out. The sorrow felt deep. It hurt him to the core of his soul. Reflections of his wrongdoing kept flashing before his eyes; in his mind. It felt as though prickly needles were jabbing at his heart.

Suddenly, he was on his knees crying out, "I'm sorry, Lord. I'm so sorry. I don't want to lie, cheat, or steal anymore to get the things I need or want. Forgive me. Help me, please!"

The more Damon cried out to God, the sorrow, guilt, and shame lifted from his heart. As he lamented, the burden of his sins vanished away. He felt revived; renewed; restored.

Damon wiped away the salty tears with Kleenex he pulled from the box on the coffee table and decided, "I'm going to get that computer programming job at Piedmont Tech Inc. in Sumnerfield.

Maybe I will run into Rayna! If it's your will, Lord."

CHAPTER 32

WHAT ARE THE ODDS?

"Ouuuuuch! Will you please watch it? Can't you see my arm is broken?" Tasha yelled at the paramedic as they were wheeling her in the hospital on the gurney.

"I'm sorry, ma'am. I'm sorry. Today's my first day on the job." The young woman said anxiously.

Tasha peered into the young woman's weary eyes and saw a reflection of herself when she was at that age. She felt apologetic and shameful for scolding her.

"It's okay, sweetie," Tasha said calmly. "The first week or so is always the hardest, but it will get better over time."

Forgetting all the pain now, Tasha filled the lady's ears with rookie stories of her first year as a nurse.

Before long, the girl didn't seem nervous any more.

"Thank you so much for your patience and understanding, Ms. Tasha. My name is Virginia, but my friends call me Jenny."

"Okay, Jenny. Don't fret. You're gonna be fine."

The intercom popped on and someone said, "Paging Dr. Saunders; paging Dr. Saunders. Can you please go to ER, room A4?"

Tasha's heart sank and her hands began to shake. The pain in her arm and shoulder worsened. She hid under the sheet like a toddler who was awaiting inoculation.

Her phone rang. She didn't look to see who was calling out of fear that it could be Raymond.

All at once, the curtain flew back! Tasha gasped in shock with the covers still pulled over her head!

"What are you doing here, John?!" she yelled.

"I beg your pardon, ma'am?" Dr. Saunders queried confusingly.

Tasha realized this voice didn't sound anything like the man she had the previous encounter with. His voice was deeper...almost like Barry White.

Slowly removing the covers from her face and examining the man from head to toe. He was average height, dark-toned, medium build, and cute.

Tasha thought to herself, "Those familiar eyes resembled someone...what are the odds?"

"Are you okay, Miss?"

"Uh—Y-yeah," she stammered. "It's just that you look like another Dr. Saunders I met today; only he was-"

"You must be talking about Rakim," he laughed.

She sat completely upright. "What? No! I'm talking about John."

"Oh! My bad...I have a brother named Rakim Saunders. I'm Hasheem. We're fraternal twins. He works here on the 2nd floor in pediatrics."

Then, she heard the intercom again, "Paging Dr. Saunders...paging Dr. Saunders. Can you please hurry to pediatrics?"

Tasha was speechless.

Finally looking at her phone, she realized the missed call was from Aunt Hilda Mae.

"Oh my goodness! The twins!" she said worriedly. "Dr. Saunders can you please hurry?! I have to get home to my children."

"I'm sorry ma'am. Is everything all right?"

"Just get the x-rays and cast me up if you need to. I gotta get home to my children!"

She grabbed her purse to get her phone to call Aunt Hilda Mae while Dr. Hasheem Saunders went to go check the x-rays.

Suddenly, a piece of paper fell to the floor. She was in too much pain to pick it up. When Dr. Saunders walked back into the room to give her the report, he noticed she was staring at the paper.

"I'll get it for you, ma'am. You'll be pleased to know that..."

"To know what?!

He stared at the paper, gazed at her and then, back at the paper.

Dr. Saunders, what is it?" she said harshly.

He flinched. "Oh, um. You have an arm fracture from the fall. We'll put a cast on it and prescribe some pain medication." Still baffled, he continued, "You'll need to follow up with your primary doctor about treatment and care."

Tasha couldn't help but feel disturbed by Hasheem's peculiar behavior concerning the piece of paper with the phone number on it.

"Well...may I please have my paper?"

Hesitantly, he glanced at it once more before passing it to her. As he was walking away slowly, he shook his head.

"Is there something else, Hasheem?"

He walked over to her and said, "I see the number you have belongs to my brother. I told you that his name is Rakim.

As he gazed into her cold, sharp eyes, he continued, "And he's married. His wife's Deana and, they have three kids."

He noticed Tasha's disappointment, embarrassment, and anger . "I'm sorry, Mrs. Brown."

Tasha rolled her eyes. "What you sorry for? Won't nobody trying to get with him. He just wanted to know how much everything cost so he could pay my medical bill. That's the only reason I have his number."

With a crackling voice now, Tasha fought back tears. "Send me the bill! Hurry up so I can get outta here!" She balled up the piece of paper.

"Okay, Mrs. Brown. I will get everything ready."

Without thinking, Hasheem held her hand and unexpectedly said, "You know, I'm a pretty good judge of character and, you seem like an intelligent woman who's just going through it right now. I can honestly say, I know what rejection feels like when you have all your eggs in one basket and the receiver doesn't want them."

She peered into his soft-spoken eyes and, the anger began to lift from her heart. Tasha could feel the kindness and genuine concern in his voice. She felt a lump swelling in her throat like a knot in a rope. She found herself crying in his arms.

CHAPTER 33

THE INTERVIEW

As Damon headed to Piedmont Tech, Inc., he was anxious to start his new journey. He saw an add online and sent his resume in. Someone from the company called him a couple of days later and asked him to come for an interview. He rehearsed for the interview several times the night before.

He thought about how he had not been to church since he was a youngster. He prayed, "Lord, please help me get this job and find a good church that I can learn more about you. If it's your will that I meet Rayna, then make it happen. In Jesus' name. Amen.

Driving a shiny, new black convertible BMW and looking like he just had a photo shoot from GQ magazine, Damon strutted into the lobby of Piedmont Tech in his pair of shiny polished black Oxfords wearing a black pin-striped Armani suit with a white shirt and white tie that had small black diagonal stripes. He felt humbled to get another shot at life.

The secretary at the front desk smiled as her eyes approved of whom was standing in front of her. He reached out to shake her hand. She said, "How may I help you?" She was so squeamish that saliva spewed from her mouth onto his hand.

He casually slid his hand from hers and smiled. Trying to ease her embarrassment, he jokingly said, "Well, I believe I will definitely get the job now, young lady, since you have anointed me with your saliva."

They both burst with laughter as he reached for the hand sanitizer on her desk. She said, "I'm so sorry. Mr. Simpson. We've been expecting you. Can this just be our inside joke, please?"

Noticing her name plate, he said, "Certainly, Mrs. Denise Laney. As long as the cameras don't mine the inside joke as well." They laughed again.

She blushed and looked him over as if he were a juicy, tantalizing, mouth-watering, thick-boned ribeye. "You know, Mr. Simpson, I really hope you do get the job here. I would definitely like to show you anything...I mean, around. And it's Ms. not Mrs." Then she winked at him.

"Um...I appreciate the information, Ms. Laney," using his professional tone with her. He walked away and took a seat.

She saw that he was disinterested in her and thought to herself, "He ain't all that, anyway. Stuck up hood rat!"

She let the interviewer know that he had arrived.

A door suddenly opened and a bald, heavy set Caucasian man stepped out and said, "Welcome, Mr. Simpson! Won't you please come in?"

As Damon was entering the office, he looked back at Ms. Laney who rolled her eyes. He pointed to the cameras and smiled.

She turned her back and started gathering papers. Damon was glad he wasn't one of those papers right now. There were a few that she crumpled up and threw in the trash.

When he sat down, Mr. Jackson told him how impressed he was with his resume.

"I see you have a Bachelor's Degree in Information Technology from the reputable Jenkins Computer Institute. I am looking to hire someone who is dedicated, has a strong knowledge of software development, and outstanding graphic design skills." Mr. Jackson cleared his throat and added, "Uh, we also would prefer someone single; which I see that you are."

Damon raised an eyebrow when Mr. Jackson mentioned someone single versus married. He knew that he wanted to get married and have a family someday; so, he interjected and said, "Excuse, Mr. Jackson, but why someone who is single instead of married? Does that mean I lose the job when I eventually get married?"

"Oh, of course not! You misunderstood me, Mr. Simpson. His cheeks turning red.

He quickly clarified by saying, "We try to divvy up the projects to accommodate the married and the single people—for their benefit. The projects here cause for long hours and travelling—mostly domestically and internationally. These projects are ideal for single folks."

Mr. Jackson further explained, "Married people are placed on projects that require only local travel and, they remain at the office more. This means they are not paid as much as the single folks; unless they request to have the bigger projects," he smiled.

Damon thought about his "second chance" at walking the straight and narrow and replied, "You know, Mr. Jackson, this job sounds almost too good to be true. What's the catch?"

"Trust me, there is nothing fishy, he laughed. "Listen, Mr. Simpson, when my grandfather started this company 20 years ago, there were only three employees—my uncle, one of my cousins, and my oldest sister. It took them five years to get this business off the ground and running. Now we are one of the top 5 AI software developers along the East Coast. We pride ourselves on hard work year round."

"So all work and no play, huh?"

"I'm not saying that. We do "play" and relax; just not as much as other companies.

"Okay. How about the benefits, here?" Damon inquired.

"The health and life insurance benefits are excellent and there are company perks that come along with the job. For example, to relocate single people, the company is willing to pay the deposit plus housing costs up to three months free in a two-bedroom townhouse of your choosing here in Sumnerfield. For married couples, it is up to six months free in a three-bedroom house or townhome. You also receive a quarterly one-week vacation to take throughout the year—unless you're on a major project."

He walked over to his office bar and grabbed some bottled water for himself and Damon.

"Oh, I almost forgot. We offer "remote" days twice a week—Mondays and Wednesdays; unless you're on a major project."

Damon sat up in his chair, and said, "Are you offering me the job, sir?"

"If you want it." he said happily. "You came highly recommended by the Institute. Graduated top of your class!"

He reached out to shake Mr. Jackson's hand, "I accept the job, Sir. When do I start?"

"Immediately after the online orientation, which is in two weeks. This will give you time to find a place and get settled in. You can talk to Ms. Laney and, she'll give you the orientation packet with all the details.

"Thank you, Mr. Jackson. I won't let you down."

"Welcome to Piedmont Tech, young man!"

CHAPTER 34

THE UNEXPECTED

Ray-Ray, please talk some sense into Raymond today! This is his final warning to leave Carol alone! She has made her decision. Now, he can either walk away or choose to be lame."

Carol rubbed James' back. "Baby, calm down. Everything's alright. I will talk to Raymond."

"The devil is a liar! Not without me you won't! Case closed."

"Dad, is there anything you want me to do? You know I got your back, right?"

"I appreciate you son, but God can back me better than anyone ever could."

Sierra looked at Benjamin's face with worry. She felt guilty for wanting to leave in the midst of all the chaos but knew it was only right to stay with him as long as he needed her to. She linked her arm in his saying, "C'mon sweetie, let's have a seat." He smiled and held her as they sat together on the couch.

Ray-Ray was pacing back and forth with anticipation as to what may take place because of Raymond's foolish pride and egomaniacal behavior.

BOOM! BOOM! BOOM! "Open up, Carol! We need to talk!"

As James peered out the window, he saw an old pickup pulling away in the distance. Loud country tunes blasting. He could see that Raymond was anxious. After putting a switchblade in his pocket, James dashed from the bedroom and flung open the door and pushed Raymond away onto the porch.

All eyes watched in silence.

"What can I do for you, Raymond?"

"Man, I need to talk to Carol!"

"Listen, Raymond, anything you have to say to Carol, you can address it to me. Now, I don't know what's going on, man, but my wife is off limits to you."

Carol stepped onto the porch and stood in front of James trying to ease the tension between him and Raymond.

Benjamin and Sierra were looking on from the living room window.

"Why are you doing this, Raymond? I want no part of whatever it is you've got going on. I am asking you to please leave our home." Carol begged.

Ray-Ray came outside and scooted around Carol. "Daddy, where's Tasha and the twins?"

Raymond began to cry and held Ray-Ray by the hands. "Baby girl, I didn't mean what I said to you earlier. You know I would never hurt you. I just wanna talk to your Mama."

Sierra brought her some tissue and returned to Benjamin's side.

Ray-Ray handed it to Raymond and said, "Don't you remember what happened between y'all Daddy? Mama did what she felt was right."

"Yeah, but... she didn't raise you. You got shipped off to your grandparents," Raymond feuded.

"Water under the bridge, Daddy. Let it go. She's moved on." Rayna reminded him.

Raymond reached passed Ray-Ray to take Carol by the hands.

James stepped in front of Ray-Ray and punched Raymond in the mouth. Raymond tumbled backwards off the porch to the ground. James reached in his pocket and pulled out the switchblade. Glances of prison bars immediately flashed before his eyes. He quickly dropped it, looked back at Carol, and said, "Please call the police and let them know there's a trespasser here and, he won't leave of his own freewill."

Benjamin and Sierra quickly ran outside.

Ray-Ray rushed over to help Raymond up. She hugged him and cried, "Daddy, can you please just leave before the cops get here?!"

"Nah, baby girl. It's too late for that. I'm just such a loser. I don't have your Mama or Tasha." He began wiping the blood from his mouth. "I'm a sorry, good-for-nothing father and husband. You know, I haven't even talked to or checked on the twins in weeks? I'm tired, Ray-Ray!"

The police arrived to see what was going on. They saw that Raymond had blood on his shirt and James and Carol were standing on the porch. Officer Whitman walked over to talk to Raymond and Officer Harris to James and Carol.

Neither parties involved wanted to press charges. The officers asked Raymond to leave.

Raymond started twirling around and around pointing up at the sky.

Officer Whitman carefully approached him. "Sir, are you okay? Do you understand me? Please leave the premises now, sir."

Raymond ignored and pretended he was shooting a gun at the clouds.

She reached for her radio asked for the Crisis Prevention Counselor and back up to come to the scene.

He looked at the officers and yelled, "Leave now! Leave now!" Falling to the ground, he felt something under his knee. He carefully slipped it in his hand.

Ray-Ray walked over to the officers feeling like she was about to have a panic attack and said, "I think my dad is having a nervous breakdown. Please, help him!" She began to sob uncontrollably.

Benjamin and Sierra dashed to comfort her.

Officer Harris radioed for an ambulance while Officer Whitman walked over to help Raymond to the car.

All of a sudden, she shrieked in pain and fell to the ground with blood gushing from her throat. James rushed over and tried to help stop the bleeding but, it was spewing out so quickly, there was nothing he could do. Officer Whitman died at the scene.

Officer Harris screamed, "Put down your weapon, sir!"

But Raymond was yelling, "I'm tired! You hear me?" And charged at Officer Harris with the switchblade in his hand.

The officer fired his weapon twice and Raymond fell to the ground face forward.

Ray-Ray and Carol both ran to him crying and holding him in their arms!

No one could believe Raymond was gone!

CHAPTER 35

REAL TALK

When Hasheem finally made it to the second floor to talk to Rakim, he saw his nephews and niece beaming with pride as they played with their father. Deana was sitting by smiling from Earth to Heaven during their family lunch date. Hasheem strolled over to speak to her while Rakim was wrestling with the kids and didn't notice he was there.

"Hey sis, how are you?"

She stood and gave him a hug. "Hi, brother. I'm doing great! It's good to see you, Hasheem. You bout married yet?" she chuckled.

"Well, if you must know, I'm married to my work and it keeps me plenty busy," he laughed.

They both watched Rakim play with the kids until they spied him out and came running over for their hugs and tickles.

"Uncle Hasheem is here!" said Dinah.

Rakim seemed surprised. "What's up man? What brings you up here? Y'all ain't busy down there in ER?"

"Now is this the way to greet your brother, baby? Come on. You guys haven't really chatted in a while." Deana noted.

"It's okay, sis. I didn't mean to intrude on your lunch date anyway."

She looked at her Samsung watch and told Hasheem it was time for them to leave anyway. They quickly hugged and kissed Rakim goodbye and sprinted off.

Rakim walked over to his desk and said, "So big bro, what's going on?"

"Hey 'real talk'; brother to brother; man to man."

"This sounds serious. You okay, Hasheem?"

"I'm fine. It's you I'm worried about lil bro."

"What for? I'm good."

"You sure? You're gonna lose your family if you don't stop with the shenanigans. I talked to this lady in ER today that had your phone number."

Rakim started pacing nervously. "Nah, it's not what you think, Hasheem. I caused her accident and told her to call me so I could pay her bill."

"Well, then why did you use the name, "John?""

"I didn't want Deana to find out."

"How dumb do you think I am, Rakim? Tasha got upset when I told her you were married, had three kids, and, I gave your real name."

Rakim became infuriated. "Why did you do that? Why you always meddling? You need to tend to your business. I can handle mine."

"It shouldn't matter, Rakim, if you were just going to pay the bill, right? Besides, she balled the paper up and said she'll pay the bill herself."

Rakim pushed Hasheem to the wall and warned him. "Stop messing in my business, man. I ain't playing with you!"

"It's not fair what you're doing to Deana and the kids. She don't deserve this crap, Rakim. Not a half nitwit like you!" Hasheem pushed him back.

"Always about Deana, huh? You still mad cause you didn't get her? Leave us alone, Hasheem. She's my wife!" Bumping his shoulder, Rakim said, "And stay away from Tasha, too!"

"Are you kidding me? You can't tell me to stay away from a woman that you shouldn't be talking to in the first place. Did you forget that I'm single and you're married? If I want to holla at Tasha, then I will!"

Rakim turned around and grabbed Hasheem by the collar of his shirt and shoved him to the floor.

An older nurse's aide was walking by and saw the scuffle. "Y'all brothers should be ashamed of yourselves. Whatever it is can't be that serious that it shouldn't wait til you get off work. Now get up from there and go to your stations. Hasheem, ain't you supposed to be in ER?"

Hasheem pushed Rakim off of him and said, "Yes, Mama Kincade. You're right." He brushed his clothes off and glared at Rakim.

Rakim walked over to Mrs. Kincade and gave her a hug. "I'm sorry, Mama Kincade."

She looked at both of them and shook her head. "Such a disgrace. Y'all are family. Don't let nothing get in the way of that. Family is important. It's everything. You don't know when it might be the last time you see each other. Is this the last memory you want to have? Rolling around and tussling on the floor like wild dogs over a bone. Apologize to each other and hug because I ain't leaving until you do."

They hugged each other and quietly agreed to square up later.

CHAPTER 36

GAINFULLY EMPLOYED

M r. Jackson escorted Damon to the front desk. "Ms. Laney will you please give Mr. Simpson the orientation packet so that he will be able to start within the next couple of weeks? Oh, and call Ms. R....I mean, Ms. Rodriguez-Ramirez to show him around and where his office is." He shook Damon's hand to welcome him again and headed back to his office.

Seeming reluctant, Ms. Laney said, "Okay, Mr. Jackson," I'll call Ms. R."

Damon saw that she was still upset with him. "Is there something wrong, Ms. Laney?"

She shoved his orientation packet towards him on the counter of her desk. "Nah, ain't nothing the matter. Here's your packet, Mr. Simpson." She said sarcastically.

"Am I missing something here? If so, please tell me so, I can rectify it. I would like for us to be able to get a long."

"Well, you made me feel like a fool with all this flirting knowing that you weren't really interested in me. I mean..."

"Hey, I apologize. That wasn't my intention. Honestly, I think you're a beautiful, young lady. There are so many guys out there around your age that would love to get to know you."

"Yeah, but the ones my age still only wanna play games—like they in high school."

"Well, have you tried going to church?"

"That's a little too boring for my taste. Church guys are so serious. They don't know how to have fun. They just wanna talk about the Lord all the time."

"I beg to differ. I recently gave my life to Christ and, I definitely don't feel I'm boring."

"Well, good for you. I hope you ain't gone act like you 'holier than thou.' I grew up going to church here at Sumnerfield Missionary Baptist Church and sometimes them folks act like they ain't never been sinners before."

Leaning on the counter of her desk now, Damon replied, "Even so, you can't let anything or anyone deter you from living for Christ. You have to give an account for you; not what others do."

"Oh, here you go; trying to 'save' somebody."

"I'm not trying to 'save' you; just wishing you would give Jesus a chance.

She looked at him with a smile and said, "Maybe, some-day."

"When does your church have services? I'm getting ready to relocate here from Charlestown."

"Oh, they have church every Sunday starting at 10:00 or 10:30? I ain't been in a while...like, a couple of years. I think Pastor Johnson retiring once they can find a new pastor. Matter of fact, Ms. R recently joined there."

Realizing she hadn't called her to take him on a tour of the building, Ms. Laney quickly picked up the phone and asked her to come down.

Damon took the packet and began looking through it.

Suddenly, an average height, pleasantly plump, brown-skinned Latino woman walked down the steps dressed in a black pant suit with a white butterfly collared shirt wearing white pumps approached him with a glowing smile.

"Hi, I'm Ms. Hazel Rodriguez-Ramirez, but you can call me, Ms. R. How are you, Mr. Simpson? "

"I'm well, Ms. R., I hope you are." He politely reached out to shake her hand and noticed an unevenly pigmented, grotesque, scar running along her hand to her wrist whispering his past.

Ms. R. felt his wondering eyes staring and quickly let go of his hand and pulled the sleeve of the suit jacket closely to the palm of her hand.

"Um, welcome to Piedmont Tech. Shall we begin the tour?"

"Yes ma'am." He turned to Denise and shook her hand. "See you around, Ms. Laney." And pointed to the camera. They both laughed.

Ms. R. didn't see what was so amusing. As they walked away, she said, "I see you've become acquainted with 'friendlier than thou'."

"Not like that. It's like I told her; I'm not interested in acquainting someone that I work with."

"Oh. Okay." She turned and asked, "Would you like to take the escalator or the elevator?"

"I prefer the elevator, please. And thank you."

They made it to the 2nd floor and, she took him to a spacious room that had a cityscape view, mini bar, balcony overlooking Sumnerfield Community Park, and expensive-looking furniture.

Damon was admiring the view from the window. He couldn't help but reflect on his past. He felt a bubble in his throat rise like a turbulent wave as his face turned warm and red. His voice cracked. "Is this my office?"

Ms. R. brought him a bottled water from his office fridge. "Yes, are you alright? Is it too small? We can get you a bigger one."

"Uh, no; I'm fine." He gushed. "This is unbelievable!"

"I know what you mean. It took a lot for me to get here, too." She lamented.

They both felt a magnetic presence as they turned to each other. Damon thought of how much Hazel reminded him of Lacy. Easy to talk to...except not quite as a sister.

And just like that, Hazel took Damon's hands and gently placed them in hers. She asked, "Do you mind if I pray for you?"

"Here? Now?" Damon looked around the office and glanced in the hallway to see if anyone was walking by. "Oh. Okay."

Unashamed and unapologetically, she prayed for him. Damon felt chills flowing throughout his body.

After the prayer was over, Rayna seemed to be an afterthought in Damon's mind.

"So where are you going to stay in Sumnerfield?" Hazel wondered.

Damon shrugged his shoulders. "I don't know anything or anyone in Sumnerfield. I'm not sure where to look."

"Well, there are some townhomes near the park. They're really nice. I can give you the number to the realtor."

Without thinking, he said, "I have a better idea. How about you show them to me?"

She kindly declined.

CHAPTER 37

DISBELIEF

O fficer Harris continued to try to stop the bleeding from Officer Whitman's throat but, James kept telling him, "She's gone, Sir. I'm sorry."

A couple of ambulances and more police arrived.

Rayna and Carol were both sobbing inconsolably as Benjamin and Sierra tried to tear them away from Raymond's bloody corpse. James ran over to hold Carol who fainted in his arms.

The familiar scene of blood, sirens, and multiple cops flooded Rayna's memory of that terrible, grim night when Elliot attempted to kill her.

Her body suddenly crumpled to the ground like a deflated balloon.

Paramedics ran to each of them; including the deceased ones on the scene. Rayna and Carol were rushed to Kelton Memorial. James accompanied Carol while Sierra rode along with Rayna. Benjamin was in tow driving his car like a NASCAR racer.

The deceased were transported for forensic autopsies to determine the cause, manner, and time of deaths.

Benjamin notified Grandma Flo and David of Raymond's demise. He also informed them to meet at Kelton Memorial because Carol and Rayna were taken to ER by medics.

Upon arrival to the hospital, Dr. Saunders and his team were prepared for each of the traumatized patients. As they brought Carol and Ray-Ray in, a nurse was finishing up Tasha's purple and red cast—Latisha and Anthony's favorite colors.

"What in the world is all the commotion?" Tasha asked the nurse.

Helping Tasha get dressed, she said, "I overheard Dr. Saunders say somebody was killed and, they brought in a couple of family members that were distraught."

Ray-Ray hollered out, "Daddy! Ooh Daddy! Bring him back, please! Dr. you have to get my Daddy and bring him back! Pleeeease!"

Carol finally came to after fainting. She was devastated and overcome with grief as she flooded James' shoulder with tears. "Raymond! Poor Raymond!"

Just then Tasha flung open the privacy curtain. The women's yelping and familiar voices guided her footsteps. She ignored her phone ringing in the distance as she grew closer to the wailing. "It can't be!" She thought. "Not my Raymond!"

Closer and closer to the screams, she ran into Dr. Saunders who saw the frightened look upon her face. "Mrs. Brown? What's wrong?"

"Get outta my way! Where is...?"

Then Tasha collapsed on the floor like a wilted flower when she saw them. Benjamin ran over to her and helped Dr. Saunders pull her limp body from the floor. Tasha began repeating the moans and groans of the grievous women.

Grandma Flo and David finally arrived. Grandma Flo's eyes were puffy clouds from numerous tears. They saw Benjamin and the Doctor trying to hold Tasha. She ran over to help. "Tasha, I'm so sorry about Raymond. I know how you feel!"

She squeezed Grandma Flo and held her tightly. "What happened to him, Ms. Flo? What happened?"

"I don't know all the details. I'll come check on you as soon as I see how Carol and Ray-Ray are doing."

Tasha became infuriated immediately! "Did it happen at their house? Carol's and James'? Is that where Raymond was?"

Grandma Flo, David, and Benjamin were bound by silence.

"Of course it was!

Grandma Flo quickly reminded her, "Sweetie, Raymond's dead. I'm ___."

"I don't care, Ms. Flo! I don't care!" Devastated, she began pounding Dr. Saunders' chest.

He motioned for a nurse to come help him get Tasha back to the room. He understood her anger, fear, and disbelief.

Grandma Flo and David went to make sure Carol and James were okay while Benjamin went to check on Sierra and Ray-Ray.

Tasha's phone rang again. She was too hysterical to answer.

After sedating her, Dr. Saunders sat with the weeping widow; without saying a word. Again, he gently held her soft, tender hand, took some tissue, from the counter, and wiped away her tears. She didn't seem to mind.

CHAPTER 38

REGRET--HIS

Rakim's shift was over and, he started packing up to go home. His hand accidentally tipped over the picture of his family. Holding it in his hands, he stared at the kids and Deana. He glided his fingers across their faces...his beautiful creations. There was no greater love Rakim ever felt than for his children.

He reflected upon the day that that photo was taken. He remembered his absence from the family photo shoot due to another young lady's presence across town at the luxurious Haymount Hotel.

His heart filled with resentment when he stared at Deana's sparkling eyes that danced with inner joy.

Rakim thought about how he regretted ever marrying Deana. So many times he wanted to tell her it was over between them. But he didn't want to abandon or become a disappointment to his children. He felt trapped...suffocated.

He sat down in his leather black office chair and pondered of ways he could dissolve their marriage due to his unhappiness. He didn't intend on marriage but, Deana had to go and get pregnant.

Frustrated now, Rakim pounded his desk. He could hear Hasheem's words saying, "You're going to lose your family!"

Returning his focus to the photo, Rakim pictured Tasha's face being there instead of Deana's. He smiled from Earth to Heaven. "I wonder if she's still here!" He sat the photo down, grabbed his things, and raced to the elevator.

When he got to ER, his ears were deafened by the howling cries. Rakim remembered his own mother's when she was told their Dad died from cardiac arrest on their 19th birthday. He shook his head in sorrow and went to the nurse's desk to see if Tasha had checked out.

"No, Dr. Saunders, she and your brother are in room A4."

Rakim's face tightened and, he clinched his fists. He walked briskly to the room and peered through the small gap of the privacy curtain. Hasheem's back was turned away from him and, Tasha was asleep. While snapping a picture of her, he noticed Hasheem was holding her hand. Instead of causing a scene, Rakim walked away and whispered to himself, "Oh, we will definitely square up later, bro!"

On his ride home, he beat the steering wheel as if it were his opponent in a boxing match. "I'll get you for this Hasheem! You know I saw her first!"

He pulled into the parking lot of Tyson's Liquor Store and spotted a tall, slender, middle-aged, bronze-skinned female getting out of her black and silver Benz. As they both walked towards the door, he said, "Let me get that for you, Queen Booty!"

"Oh, you're more than welcome to get it, King Snake!"

They both shared a hearty laugh, bought their favorite adult beverage, and headed for Haymount Hotel.

By the time Rakim arrived home, the kids were asleep and Deana was sitting in the den watching a movie.

"What are you still doing up? You don't have to wait up for me. I'm a grown man." Rakim raged.

"C'mon baby. I just wanna watch this movie, alright?"

"Whatever! It's probably about *"How to Get Rid of Your Husband!"*

"Can you please keep your voice down, Rakim, before you wake the kids?"

"The kids, the kids...that's all you care about!" he sputtered.

Deana sat in silence and turned the volume up a little.

"Oh you better turn that down! You might 'wake the kids'," he said sarcastically and continued, "You know what, Deana, I'm so sick of this. I'm tired of you!" Staggering away, he shouted out, "I'm gone sleep in the guest room tonight!"

When Rakim went to take a shower, he scrolled on his phone to find the picture of his 'sleeping beauty.' He imagined bathing with Tasha. Caressing his body all over. Up and down. He envisioned the two of them making love with the steam rising between their heated bodies. Fulfilling each other's desires. Overcome with excitement, he relieved himself in the shower.

He went downstairs to get some water and glanced in the den. He saw Deana cuddled with a box of tissue as she lay across the white leather couch.

On his way past the door heading back upstairs, he laughed.

CHAPTER 39

MIXED FEELINGS

D amon returned to Charlestown excited about his new journey and second chance. He settled on the couch after getting a bottled water and turned on the local news.

"There was a police shooting today in Kelton, NC at the home of Pastor James Nolan, Sr. and his wife, Carol Nolan. Apparently, police were called out to a domestic dispute where the suspect, Raymond Anthony Brown, was trespassing on Pastor Nolan's property and would not leave. Two officers from the Kelton Police Department came and Mr. Brown was asked to leave the premises. The suspect had an altercation with Officer Whitman killing her on the scene. Mr. Brown was shot and killed by Officer Harris who has been released from his duties pending further investigation. This is standard procedure when an officer is involved in a shooting. Officer Carla Whitman is survived by her husband, Officer Sebastian Whitman; their 3-year old daughter, Kaitlyn Whitman; and 5-year old son, Randy Whitman. The suspect is survived by his wife, Tasha Brown; their 10-year old twins, Latisha and Anthony Brown; and his 30-year old daughter, Rayna Jennings-Nolan, from a previous relationship with Carol Nolan. Prayers are needed for all parties involved..."

Damon jumped up from the couch frantically. "It can't be!" he shouted. His heart pounded heavily and a feeling of uneasiness overshadowed him. He began pacing back and forth. "That's Pastor Nolan! Elliot killed his family!"

He really needed to talk to Lacy. Damon went to bed wrestling with his thoughts throughout the night.

Retrieving another bottle of water from the kitchen, Damon noticed a Bible he recently purchased standing in the corner of a shelf. He remembered at checkout the cashier said, "When you can't sleep, get your Bible and read Psalm 91, then pray. God is trying to tell you something."

"Let me try that," he thought to himself. He carefully turned the thin pages until he reached Psalm 91.

When he got to verse : '[15] He shall call upon me, and I will answer him: I will be with him in trouble; I will deliver him, and honour him,' this scripture pricked his heart. He fell to his knees and prayed, "Lord, I can't call Lacy or talk to her right now; so, I'm asking YOU to guide my path. I pray I make the right decision about talking to Pastor Nolan. If it's YOUR will. Continue to teach me your Word. In Jesus' name. Amen."

He sat in the worn-out black leather recliner and watched the old movie, *"Escape From Alcatraz."*

The beaming sunlight slowly climbed above the clouds, peeped through the blinds of the living room window, and awakened Damon from a deep sleep. He embarrassingly wiped the drool from his mouth, washed his hands, and made some coffee.

Turning to the local news for an update about yesterday's shooting, it was only a repeat. Nothing new.

Damon thought about staying in Sumnerfield for a couple of days to find a place and then start packing to move.

As he looked around the small, cozy cabin, he discovered there wasn't much worth or of any value to take with him. Thanks to his well-paid salary, he can afford nicer things. He decided to donate the items to the homeless shelter where he and his Mom once stayed for a couple of months when he was 7 years old. She owed a gambling debt and couldn't pay the rent...again.

He couldn't wait to stop by Piedmont Tech and get the number to the realtor from Hazel!

CHAPTER 40

LIARS!

The sounds of snoring awakened Tasha from her slumber. She smiled as she stared at Hasheem trying to rest sitting in the small office chair. His head nodding back and forth. She sat up to touch his shoulder but realized her hands were drizzled with drool. Embarrassed, Tasha quickly swiped the towel lying on the bed and wiped her hands and said, "Good morning, Dr. Saunders. Am I free to go?"

A startled Hasheem, quickly said, "Um, yes. You're ready. I will grab your paperwork." He ran into the trash can on his way out nearly tripping. He asked shyly, "Can I get you some coffee?"

"No thanks, I need to get to my kids to tell 'em about their Daddy."

Hasheem saw the dread in her eyes. "Do you mind if I call you to check on you?"

Tasha heard the sincerity in his voice and felt he genuinely cared. "Sure, that's fine." she smiled.

A warm feeling of peace overcame Hasheem. "Okay, let me get those papers now."

Everyone checked out and gathered for a meeting in the parking lot. They hugged each other and shared tears at the loss of Raymond.

James said, "You know, we really need to check on each other often. We are living in a time where the Devil is doing everything he can to keep us from serving God. He is attacking our minds. I feel a little responsible because I let flesh override my spirit. I should have talked to Raymond; find out what was really going on with him."

Tasha interrupted, "It wouldn't have mattered, Pastor. Raymond has been suffering from anxiety, depression, and schizophrenia for a while. He wouldn't take his meds on a regular basis, or go to therapy, and stopped reading the Bible. I don't think there's anything any of us could have really done to ease his unhappiness."

"Yeah, James, don't take on the guilt. Daddy chose not to get the help from God or from us." Ray-Ray gave him a hug.

Carol went over to Tasha and hugged her. "If you need anything, please let us know, okay?"

Tasha turned to James and said, "Pastor Nolan, I would like for the funeral to be at your church. I don't know about the eulogy. If everyone who knew him could just say some kind words about him, I would appreciate it."

"Sure, Sister Brown." Pastor Nolan agreed.

Tasha asked nervously. "Ray-Ray, can you please come with me to tell the twins?"

Not really wanting to, Ray-Ray concurred. "Let me go shower and change and come right over."

"Thank you so much."

On the ride home, Tasha felt guilty for feeling relieved that Raymond died. She knew in her heart they were headed for divorce and, based on his obsession with Carol, he was already causing problems. Either way, the twins were bound to receive dreadful news.

She jumped when her phone rang but felt too tired to answer. Before pulling into the driveway, she checked the voicemail and it said Raymond's body had been released and she could have his body picked up from the morgue along with his belongings and paperwork.

Tasha called Locklear's Funeral Home to pick up the body. Looking at the calendar, she decided to have the funeral on the following Tuesday...5 more days.

The twins ran out to greet her. "What happened to your arm, Mommy?" Latisha was curious.

"Look, Tisha, Mom has our favorite colors on her cast!" Anthony added excitedly.

Latisha argued, "Is that all you care about, Ant-Man? Mommy is hurt!"

Aunt Hilda Mae joined in, "Children, hush that fuss and let your Mama get in the house." She hugged Tasha and told the children to get her things from the car.

She helped Tasha inside and began to cry. "Lord, my Raymond is gone!"

"Yeah, Tasha said sadly, "Ray-Ray is coming over so we can tell the kids together."

"Alright. Good." Aunt Hilda Mae said drying her eyes.

"What's wrong, Aunt Hilda?" Anthony asked and went over to hug her.

"Where's Daddy, Mommy. Why's he not with you?"

"Latisha, Can you and Anthony please go put Mommy's things in her room?" Aunt Hilda ushered them towards Tasha's bedroom.

Ray-Ray suddenly pulled up. The closer she walked towards the door, the more uncomfortable she felt. Her heartbeat was thumping so rapidly as she knocked on the door. Aunt Hilda Mae welcomed her with open arms, and they cried together.

The twins came rushing in yelling, "Rayna, Rayna! We're glad to see you!" And they hugged her tightly.

Rayna cried even harder. Tasha came out of the living room and asked everyone to come sit down. The twins were looking at everyone crying; including their Mom now.

Anthony noticed his Dad was missing. "Hey, where's Daddy?"

Latisha was crying as well. "I want Daddy. Rayna, have you seen him?"

Tasha knelt in front of them and said, "I'm sorry kids, but your Dad will not be coming home. anymore. He passed away."

Ray-Ray knelt beside her. "Daddy was sick, guys."

Anthony jumped up and ran to his bedroom slamming the door. "Liars! You're all liars!" he shouted.

Aunt Hilda Mae ran to his room to talk with him.

Latisha was crying hysterically and Ray-Ray held her. Tasha sat beside them trying to figure out what to say...how to comfort them.

Her phone rang but, she did not answer.

CHAPTER 41

SOUSE

Hasheem was smiling from Earth to Heaven and, his heart was beaming with joy as he pulled into the driveway. He hopped out the car whistling and dancing until his phone rang.

"Hello, dear! How are you?"

The woman's voice sounded shaky. She began to cry.

"What's wrong? Are the kids alright?"

Still crying, she managed to say, "Yes."

"Well, what's the matter, Deana?"

"Rakim and I had a fight last night and, he slept in the guest room. When I got up this morning, he was gone!"

"That's because he's probably at work, sis."

Deana was frantic. "No, Hasheem. I've already called and, Nurse Grantham said he's not there."

"Okay, calm down. Let me change and, I will be right over."

Hasheem quickly showered and got dressed. Grabbing the keys off the counter, he was walking out the door when Rakim pulled in the driveway.

"Rakim, what's going on with you? Deana just called here all upset. You need to ____..."

"Can we go inside, please?" Rakim asked while noticing a couple of neighbors come out to sit on their porches.

Hasheem noticed he was wreaking of booze. "Yeah. C'mon, man."

When Rakim staggered by him, Hasheem helped him up the steps into the living room.

Rakim plopped down on the couch and mumbled, "It's over, bruh!"

Hasheem went into the kitchen to make coffee. "What are you talking about?"

"Look, I confess, man. I never really wanted her, Hasheem. She just had to go and get pregnant. Why didn't she just get rid of it when I begged her to."

Bringing him a cup of black coffee, Hasheem's phone rang again.

"Hi, Deana. Yeah, he's over here. I'll send him home after he sobers up."

"Oh no you won't! Rakim shouted out. "I'm leaving you, Deana!"

"What did he say, Hasheem? Did he say he's leaving me?"

"Listen, Deana. Let me talk to him. He's drunk right now?"

"This early in the morning? It ain't even 10:00! She said angrily. "You know, he's been doing that a lot lately."

"Yeah, it reminds me of his college days." Rakim took off his shirt and laid back on the couch. "I'll call you later, sis."

"Okay, please keep me posted. I'm so confused right now."

"You and me both." Hasheem sighed.

Rakim began to snore.

Hasheem just shook his head. He took Rakim's Air Jordan's off and covered him up with the plush, fleece blanket. Then he headed over to talk to Deana.

The kids ran out to greet him, "Uncle Hasheem!"

He hugged and tickled each of them. Deana came out with tissue in hand. Her eyes were swollen like puffy clouds. She wrapped her arms tightly around Hasheem and leaned into his chest sobbing loudly.

"What's wrong, Mommy?" Dinah tugged on her shirt.

Hasheem walked Deana into the house and the kids followed like little ducklings. He helped her to the couch and ordered the kids some pizza and drinks from Door Dash. The kids ran into the den to play until it arrived.

Hasheem went into the kitchen to get her some water. "Sis, what happened between you two last night? He's talking about leaving you!"

"But I don't know what for, Hasheem? I do everything he asks. I make sure the house is clean, bills are paid, kids are taken care of, sex when he wants it. Which hasn't been lately. I don't even question him when he hangs out all times of night or stays off from home."

"Wait! What? Not coming home?" Hasheem began pacing and tapping his fist into his hand. "But, you seem so happy in public. I thought things were fine between you guys. I mean, the kids are happy every time I see them!"

"That's the thing," she sighed, "Gotta keep up public appearances. The girls in my family were taught 'having half a man is better than having no man at all.' My Mom shared my Dad with his mistress for years. That heifer even had the nerve to show her face at the funeral—crying all over his dead body."

Hasheem looked deeply into her eyes. Seeing her pain, he hugged her tightly and, she gently wrapped her hands around his neck and held on. It felt good to be this close to a woman again...even for a second Hasheem thought. He wished it was Tasha he was holding right now.

The door dasher pulled up with the pizza and drinks. Hasheem quickly released her as the kids rushed in and sat at the table waiting impatiently to receive their first slice.

Deana smiled as she watched Hasheem set the table filling each plate with pizza and their cups with orange soda. She began to think about what could've been had she chosen Hasheem. He probably would have aloud her to pursue her dream as a geographer—living abroad. She envisioned him having a clinic while she's off on archeological digs; searching for artifacts. She snapped back into reality when Hasheem started talking.

"So how long has Rakim been doing this, Deana?" he asked curiously.

"About a month or two now. Why?"

"Just wondering that's all. Don't worry. I will send him home tomorrow." He hugged her and the kids.

On the ride home, he had a pretty good idea why Rakim was behaving irrationally.

CHAPTER 42

LET'S DO IT!

Benjamin and Sierra went back to Carol and James' house along with Grandma Flo and David to help them clean up. Everyone was so exhausted from the tragic event that stemmed from Raymond's misapprehension that they forgot about the blissful couple's engagement announcement.

On arrival, they saw that the yellow and black striped caution tape had been removed but, the bloody stains still covered portions of the sidewalk and the front yard. The men helped the ladies into the house and went back outside.

James was already on the phone calling a group from his church that owned a cleaning service. As they sat quietly on the porch looking around at the turmoil, he said, "You know, I understand Raymond's plight."

Stumped, Mr. David said, "Are you alright, James?"

"Yeah, Dad." Benjamin sounded annoyed, "This man came at you trying to take your wife; yet, you understand him?"

"Well, guys, once a man's eyes become open to the truth of their past mistakes—about the temptations that misguided their judgement. It's only natural for them to seek out the treasure they lost. I hate Raymond had to die as a result. It must have been horrible for him to carry such an unbearable weight these past few years—wanting her so badly; knowing he couldn't have her."

"You a good one, Pastor, cause ain't no way I'm feeling sorry for the fool that tried to take my beloved."

"Me neither, Pop David," Benjamin chimed in.

James spoke sermonically, "That's why flesh has to die daily; so, that we are able to pray and forgive our enemies as God does the same for us."

The cleanup crew arrived and began taking out all sorts of equipment. James went to talk to the gentleman who carried a notepad in hand and a pen stashed behind his ear.

The ladies came out to bring their husbands some sweet tea and to sit with them. Sierra cozied up to Benjamin as Grandma Flo did the same with Mr. David.

Carol anxiously awaited James' return who noticed they came on the porch. She couldn't wait to lay in his arms where she felt the most peace and comfort. When she looked around the yard, she felt eerie—cold. Her body began to tremble.

"What's the matter, Carol?" James rushed to her side.

"I don't know if I'll be able to stay here, James. I can't..."

"No worries, baby, I understand. So, is this a restart or new start?" James asked.

Carol laid on his broad, burly chest and said, "Let's do a new start and continue what we have. No need to restart anything." She looked into his teary eyes and said with a radiant smile, "I love you so much, James Nolan."

"Back at ya, Mrs. Nolan."

"Are y'all gone move, Dad?" Benjamin sounded like a little kid excited about getting a puppy.

"Well, son. I guess so. We will have to figure out where to though." He held Carol's soft, tender chin in the palm of his hands and said, "Stay in Kelton closer to the church or...?"

Before he could finish, Carol shouted, "Sumnerfield near the park!"

Sierra interrupted, "Carol! That's perfect. Pastor Johnson is retiring and looking for a candidate!"

Benjamin kissed her forehead and said, "Baby, let them figure it out. I think it's time for us to be heading back."

Shyly, she looked at them and said, "Forgive me Carol and James, if I overstepped." She turned to Benjamin and kissed his chiseled cheek. "You're right, sweetie. Let's go."

With that they hugged everyone goodbye and left. It wasn't long after that Grandma Flo and David did the same.

Any heartwarming memories James and Carol had were nullified due to the tragic events that transpired. Home would never be the same. James and Carol went back inside and walked into each room of the house; including the garage. They couldn't wait to start anew and agreed to put the house on the market versus renting it out.

Carol rubbed his back on the way to the living room to sit on the couch. He used her lap as a plush, soft pillow and began to fall asleep as she gingerly massaged his scalp. Then her phone rang.

"Yes, Sierra?"

"Hey, Benji and I are going to the Justice of Peace tomorrow and would like for you and James to be our witnesses, please?"

"Already? Didn't you just get engaged?"

Benjamin interjected, "Carol, when you know...you just know. Sierra and I are in love and definitely love each other!

I asked her what did she think about going to the J-O-P and, she said, 'Let's do it!'

"Congratulations, guys! We'll be there!"

Hanging up the phone, Carol thought, "I hate Pastor Johnson is retiring but, this might be a blessing in disguise. Maybe we can spend a few days in Sumnerfield to look at houses and talk to Pastor Johnson."

James curled himself around her body and nestled his head in her breasts while she continued massaging his scalp.

CHAPTER 43

REGRET--HERS

When Hasheem left, guilt and shame overcame Deana for wanting him to hold her longer—possibly make love to her. She sensed his heartbeat was synchronizing to the beat of hers.

The cries for "more pizza" interrupted her immoral thoughts as she ran in the kitchen to carry out the kids' wishes.

Jaheem noticed her eyes brimming with tears and was immediately filled with worry. "What's wrong, Mommy? Did you and Daddy have another fight? I heard you guys last night. Why was Daddy saying all those mean things to you?"

She looked into Jaheem's fretful eyes and said, "You know, lil man, you're really growing up but, don't you worry. This is a grownup matter and, me and your Daddy will figure it out. You just focus on being a kid. Mommy and Daddy are going to do everything to make sure you guys are happy and safe." She hugged and kissed all of them and went on the patio.

She began to reminisce when she first saw Hasheem in the courtyard during her college days. Always dressed casual and wearing those round-lensed glasses with gold trimming.

Not unattractive; but cute. Nice medium build—not necessarily a hunk compared to Rakim. Seemed to be a little too laid back for anyone's taste.

He had knelt in a corner of the courtyard to tie his shoe when he sprinted over to lift her geography book from the pavement and invited her to the *Crab Shack*.

After leaving the *Crab Shack* that night because of all the arguing, Rakim came over to the dorm to apologize for his behavior. It seemed so genuine. He kept pestering me to go out with him. So I did. He was such a gentleman at first. We would talk about each other's dreams for hours when we'd go to the beach. Rakim wanted to open his own pediatric clinic someday while I was going to start a career in urban and regional planning to help with transportation and infrastructure needs. We even had a beach wedding.

"Boy did I make the wrong choice," she muttered.

I should have paid attention to those red flags my auntie had told me about. I wound up getting pregnant right before both our graduations and, he wanted me to get rid of it! I told him that it was against my moral values. We split up for about 6 weeks. And just like that, he showed up at my parents' house crying and begging for forgiveness.

Of course, my Mom said, "Girl, you betta put aside that pride and marry that man. He a doctor too. It's better to have half a man than no man at all. So what if he left you barefoot and pregnant. He came back; didn't he? Give him a chance."

The kids interrupted her train of thoughts again as they ran outside to play on the trampoline. While watching them play, the words echoed in her ear, "Give him a chance."

The thought of Hasheem crossed her mind and she wondered, "Should I give him a chance? He's always had feelings for me. And the kids love him to death."

CHAPTER 44

TASHA'S REACTION

Ray-Ray took Latisha and Anthony to the treehouse in the back yard while Tasha was on the phone setting up funeral arrangements. The twins didn't really feel like playing. They sat with her—leaning on each shoulder, silently crying.

"Guys, we're gonna get through this. Daddy would want us to." Ray-Ray tried to comfort them.

"But what happened to him?" Anthony queried.

She looked at each of them and asked, "How old are you guys now? 8 or 9?"

Latisha smiled and nudged her. "C'mon sis, you know we are ten years old?"

"Okay. You're old enough to know the truth. I won't lie to you." Rayna held them both close to her and breathed heavily. She said slowly, "Daddy was confused and sick. When he didn't take his medication, it made him think unhappy thoughts and see things that were not real."

"Like what?" Anthony interrupted.

"Well, he thought that my Mom was his wife instead of Tasha. He was so confused guys. He needed his medication."

Now Latisha seemed offensive. "Well, why didn't you or Mommy give it to him?"

Tasha entered the treehouse and sat beside them. Taking Latisha in her arms, she cried, "We tried to baby, but your Daddy didn't like the medication anymore."

Ray-Ray touched her shoulder and they looked into each other's eyes with agreement to continue. "You see guys, Daddy, had a sickness in his brain. He needed medication to help him." And she started crying.

"It's okay, Ray-Ray," Tasha continued, "I'll tell them." She grabbed them by their hands and said, "Your Daddy was shot and killed this afternoon by a police officer because he harmed another police officer."

The twins cried even harder. Ray-Ray held Anthony while Tasha held Latisha.

Aunt Hilda Mae could hear the howling from indoors and came out to help but joined instead. When everyone was done drowning in their tears, they went back inside.

Latisha and Anthony went into the den to watch TV with Aunt Hilda Mae while Tasha and Ray-Ray began tidying up the house. Afterwards, they went to the sunroom—glass of red wine in hand.

Tasha opened up to Ray-Ray about the goings on between her and Raymond. She explained how unhappy Raymond was with the marriage and confused most of the time about his love for her and for Carol. "I couldn't take his roller coaster of emotions, Ray-Ray. When he stopped taking the medication, he was unbearable to live with. If it hadn't been for Aunt Hilda Mae living with us, I believe he would have hurt me, the kids, and possibly your Mom."

"Oh, c'mon Tasha. I know Daddy was a little unstable but I don't think he would have done anything that serious."

"You didn't see those demonic eyes, Ray-Ray. The way his face became enraged with anger. Sometimes transforming into another being almost. Like he had a demonic spirit."

"Yeah but, I still can't believe Daddy would hurt you guys like..."

"Like the way he cut that police officer's throat!" Tasha glared at her.

Ray-Ray was in tears just thinking back to that moment and apologized to Tasha. "I'm sorry, Tasha, for what Daddy put you through. It seems a lot like some of the things Elliot..."

"Don't talk about it, Ray-Ray, unless you're ready."

"He took my baby, Tasha, and, he almost killed me! If Sierra and Benjamin hadn't showed up that night, I wouldn't be here talking to you right now. Domestic violence is real. It's not just physical either. He put me through it emotionally, economically, and verbally. Half the time I didn't know if I was coming or going." Ray-Ray's crying inconsolably. Tasha passes her some tissues and brings her another glass of wine.

"Listen, Ray-Ray, it looks like God has delivered us both from a lot of abuse, toxicity, and anguish. After the funeral next week, I'm going to start therapy and counseling for me and the kids. Are you still in therapy, Ray-Ray?"

"Yeah. And taking medication too."

"Good." Tasha took her by the hand and said, "You know, Ray-Ray, hopefully we can heal together."

"I would like that very much." Reluctantly, she turned to Tasha and asked, "Can Mama be a part of this healing journey?"

Tasha smiled, "She sure can! Maybe we can work on putting together a non profit or a podcast!"

Shocked at Tasha's reaction, Ray-Ray was enthused to share.

"I'm way ahead of you, Tasha! We'll talk about it once we get through this." She jumped up and hugged Tasha tightly. "Thank you so much, you don't know how much this means to me. You truly were a blessing to my Daddy."

Tasha felt so proud and, she lit up with joy. "Yes! And I've gained a bonus daughter!"

Aunt Hilda Mae came in uninvitedly and took a seat. The twins had fallen asleep on the couches in the den.

"Alright, Ray-Ray, I hope you know we ain't gone let you go back tonight. So, go on and get settled in Latisha's room."

Ray-Ray knew there was no need to argue with her and kindly accepted.

On her way to the bathroom, Tasha's phone rang.

CHAPTER 45

COMMONALITIES

The sign read: "Welcome to Sumnerfield." Damon felt relieved and at peace with finally getting his life on track. The straight and narrow from here on out. He checked in at the prestigious Regal Hotel and unpacked. When he finished, he walked out on the balcony facing the park and envisioned himself on morning jogs. He knew exactly where he hoped to find a house—townhouse! He quickly headed for Piedmont Tech.

"You back already, Brother Simpson?" Denise said sarcastically.

"Yes, Sister Laney. I am," he smiled. "Is Ms. R available?"

Denise studied Damon's face as though she were decrypting a message. "Let me check." She scrolled through her screen and said, "She's free til 1:00."

"Awesome! Will you let her know I'm here, please?"

"Y'all goin' on a lunch date?"

"C'mon, Ms. Laney," Damon chuckled.

"Listen! Cut the crap with all your professionality and just call me Denise."

Damon tried easing the tension and said, "Lil sis, why you trippin'. I want us to be friends, okay?"

Seeing that he was sincere and the fact that her only brother accidentally drowned, she folded. "Alright—big bruh!" They both laughed and she called Ms. R who said it was okay for him to come to her office.

Damon was excited about having to see Hazel again. As he bounced up the steps, he swiped a vase of flowers from someone's desk to give to Hazel. Immediately, he was reminded not only by the cameras but, also, by a 'still, small voice' that echoed in his ear, "Thou shall not steal." Without hesitation, he turned around and placed it back.

An older Caucasian lady walked up and scoffed at him. Looking embarrassed, he said, "Oh, it fell on the floor and, I just picked it up and placed it back. Once again, here comes that 'still, small voice' crying out, "Lying lips are an abomination to the Lord..." Feeling condemned, Damon changed his tune. "You know what? The truth is, I was going to take it to Ms. R. I apologize for the little white lie."

The lady became offensive, "Excuse me, young man!"

Damon knew he was digging himself in a hole and had to react quickly. "Ma'am, can I just pay you for the flowers? I just wanted to impress Ms. R. That's all," he pled.

Recognizing his good faith, she said, "Go ahead and take the flower. You owe nothing. Lord knows Ms. R. could use some kindness in her life right now."

"Thank you so much, ma'am," he breathed a sigh of relief.

"Who are you?" she asked nosily.

He smiled, "I just got hired to work in engineering; software developer. I'm Damon Simpson."

"Oh! I'm Carrie Morgan. How'd you land that job? My nephew applied a month ago and didn't even get a call for an interview."

One hand lifted high toward Heaven, he said, "God's favor and hard work!"

Placing the flower back on her desk, he walked over to Hazel's office and tapped on her door. She was busy with work and continued without breaking a stare from her computer.

"Uhm...uhm!" He tapped again.

Startled, she grinned shyly and said, "Oh! Hi, Mr. Simpson. What can I help you with?"

"Well, how are you, Ms. R?"

"I'm fine. I hope you are."

"Yes. I am as well. Thank you." He looked around her office and noticed there were no family pictures. Just a lot of beautiful paintings and books. He saw a copy on her desk of one of Maya Angelou's infamous stories, *I Know Why the Caged Bird Sings.*"

Thinking to himself, he realized they have similar taste in literature, art, and religion. What else? He wondered.

"Excuse me, Mr. Simpson, I am rather busy. Is there something you need?"

"I'm sorry. Uh, I needed the number of the realtor so that I can go ahead and look for a place. "

She reached in her desk and pulled out a purple and black business card and handed it to him. It read: "Royal Realty Properties, Inc." He looked it over and put it in his wallet.

Using a "mother's" tone, she said, "Don't lose it, now."

Smiling from Earth to Heaven, he winked at her and said, "Maybe I wouldn't if you come with me."

Hazel blushed. "Sorry, I have a meeting at 1:00."

Speaking professionally, Damon said, "Ms. R. I apologize for being too forward. I will let you get back to work. See you after orientation."

She walked him to the hallway, told him good-bye, and closed her door.

As he passed her office window, she sat at her computer and continued working. If those keys were tomatoes, that keyboard would be ladled with tomato soup.

CHAPTER 46

CONFESSION TIME

Finding the courage to finally call Tasha, Hasheem was equally nervous as if he was a college kid again. He couldn't wait to hear her voice! The phone rang three times and, he was about to hang up when he heard, "Hello?"

"Tasha, hi, it's Hasheem. Are you busy?"

"Hello, Hasheem. No. The kids are napping. How are you?"

"Never mind me. That's why I'm calling you. How you doing—considering the circumstances?"

She went outside to the patio as she whisked past Aunt Hilda Mae who muttered, "Who that?" Tasha ignored and took a seat on the A-frame swinging seat.

"I'm doing fine. Thanks for asking. Ray-Ray and I told the kids. As expected, they didn't take it well."

"Ray-Ray?" Hasheem sounded suspicious.

"Oh, Rayna! Their older sister from one of Raymond's previous relationships."

With a sigh of relief in his voice, Hasheem could smile again. "Is she going to stay with you guys for a little while?"

"She's going home tomorrow to get some clothes so she can stay until the funeral is over."

"So, you've made arrangements, huh?"

"Yeah, it's next Tuesday. I mean, all his family is here and, I want to get the kids in counseling and myself in therapy."

"That's awesome, Tasha. 'Time heals all wounds,' that's what my Mama used to say, God rest her soul."

"Sorry about that, Hasheem."

"Nah, that's okay. It's been about 7 years ago since we lost her to ovarian cancer. Hey, if you need a counselor or a good therapist, I know a few people."

"Thanks but, I'm going to go with Ray-Ray's suggestion. Her best friend is a counselor in Sumnerfield and, I'll probably go with to the therapist that she goes to as well."

"Alright. I just want you to know that I'm here if you need me, Tasha."

"I really appreciate that, Hasheem."

He heard the shower stop and came inside the house. Walking past the bathroom as Rakim was opening the door wrapped in a waist towel, Hasheem asked, "Hey, Tasha, is it okay if I call you next week after the funeral?"

"Sure. That's fine!" she said gladly not knowing Hasheem had her on speaker phone.

Rakim got dressed and stared at the mirror in the guest room. He picked up a chair and threw it. Glass shattering, Hasheem came running and opened the door.

"Fool, what's wrong with you?"

Rakim charged at him and started punching Hasheem like a wild animal out of a cage all the way into the kitchen. Once Hasheem made it to his feet, he picked Rakim up and body slammed him onto the kitchen table. He pounced on Rakim like a lion on a wildebeest. They finally quit tussling when their mother's picture crashed to the floor as if she was telling them to ""Stop that fighting!"

Both men perspiring and breathing heavily, scrambled to their feet and sat on the couch. Rakim muttered, "Sorry, man! I'll pay for the damages. I just—-I just..." and he began to cry.

Hasheem placed his hand on Rakim's shoulder, "It's alright man. You got a lot going on, bruh. Talk to me, Rakim."

Rakim calmed down and picked up the shattered picture of their mom. "All our lives, man, I felt overshadowed by you. You were Mom's favorite. I could see it in her eyes."

"Just like you were Dad's."

"I've been jealous of you for so long Hasheem."

"Jealous of me? You're the handsome one!"

"Yeah, but you got all the senses of a genius! I had to cheat, study longer, and harder than you to become a doctor. And you know what? I don't even like doing it. The only reason I chose this stupid field is because I overheard you and Mom talking about your dreams. I thought she would love me just as much if I followed suit."

"Man, she did love you, Rakim. You were just so stubborn like Daddy and, it agitated her."

"Ah, Daddy, just spoke his mind."

"That too but, he was still stubborn. If he would've taken his heart medications like he was supposed to, he probably would've lived longer."

"Maybe." Rakim shrugged. He looked around at the mess and said, "You know, I'm sorry about..."

"Is it because I was talking to Tasha? Tell the truth." Hasheem blurted out.

Rakim stood up and walked to the door. Looking out the window, he shamelessly mumbled, "Yeah. But you know, Hasheem, I don't even want her. I just wanted to annoy you. Like I did with Deana. I don't want her either...just my kids."

Hasheem motioned for him to help him pick up the broken pieces and asked, "Well, what do you want, Rakim? You seem so angry and unhappy. What do you want to do with yourself?"

"I don't wanna tell you because you might laugh."

"I won't, man, I promise. Unless it's a circus clown or a bouncer or something." An explosion of laughter filled the room.

"Nah, it's a firefighter. I've already signed up at the academy and going to do an advance training for hazardous materials afterwards."

"What about Deana and the kids?"

"What about her? I only want my kids, man."

"You can't take the kids from her man. You can't take care of them like that; especially, if you gone be fighting fires all times of day and night! You know it's best for them to stay with her."

"I'm not talking about taking them away from her—completely; I want joint custody."

Hasheem stared at him and thought about some of the things that Deana had shared with him; sleeping in the guest room, hanging out all night, and sometimes not coming home. So he asked bluntly, "Are you seeing someone else, Rakim?"

He wouldn't answer Hasheem. Instead, he went to the bathroom to take another shower and change clothes.

Rakim's phone rang and Hasheem rushed over to the kitchen island to see who was calling.

"Zara?"

CHAPTER 47

SOMETHING BORROWED & BLUE

Waking up from a car-ride nap, Carol saw familiar territory. Looking out the window, the sign read: "Welcome to Sumnerfield." She quickly leaned on James' shoulder and said, "How you doing, baby?"

"I'll always be fine as long as I have you, Carol." His tender lips soothed her forehead with a kiss.

"Do you wanna stay at Mama's or the Regal?"

"Well, we don't wanna keep them up with all our noise, do we?" he said flirtingly.

Carol blushed. "The Regal it is, lover man! She grabbed her phone to make reservations and noticed the time. "Hey babe, we need to hurry if we want to make it to the Justice of Peace on time."

The anxious couple had called each of them several times to see if they were in town yet.

James went on the balcony after tipping the bellhop once the bags were unloaded. Admiring the view that was facing the park, Carol snatched him by the hand and rushed him to the shower. When finished, they got dressed and headed over to the J-O-P.

Before going into the courthouse, Carol turned to James and said, "You know baby, I hope we find something before we have to leave for the funeral. I know we go meet with Pastor Johnson after everything's over."

James reassured her that God will work everything out for everyone's good. He helped her out of the car—hand in hand—and, they walked into the courthouse.

Staring at the rings, Benjamin was standing alone nervously waiting for Sierra to return from the bathroom. James and Carol burst through the doors each carrying a small bag in hand as Sierra reappeared and graciously wandered over to Benjamin's side.

"You guys! You need something borrowed and something blue!" Carol reached in the small bag and pulled out a pair of blue diamond earrings and James pulled out a pair of blue cufflinks. The coupled smiled with joy as they put them on.

James reached in his pocket and pulled Benjamin to the side. Tears running down his face, he said, "Son, this is James Jr.'s watch they found from the fire. I want you to keep it."

"Dad, you don't have to part with this."

"Please, Ben, I'd rather you have it." James hugged him and walked him over to Sierra who was receiving a white embroidered handkerchief from Carol.

Someone came out to let them know it was time to get started. Benjamin turned to Sierra and grinning from Earth to Heaven said, "Well, when we come through these doors again, we will be Mr. and Mrs. Benjamin Robert Murphy." He placed her arm in his and escorted her in.

The ceremony was so beautiful. You could feel the joy—the love. Everyone laughed when James pretended he misplaced the rings.

Walking down the steps of the courthouse, Benjamin and Sierra were overjoyed with wedding bliss. They hugged James and Carol and thanked them for being there.

"Hey, enjoy yourselves on your honeymoon, guys." James said proudly.

Both of them looked sneakily at each other and laughed. James and Carol were confused and begged them to share.

Benjamin explained to them that the unplanned, fast-track wedding didn't include a honeymoon package.

Sierra went on to say, "Yeah, and since we are getting ready to move into our new home, we will need to move all 'honeymoon' finances to our emergency fund. Now that we're married, we have to be good stewards of our money."

"Absolutely, wifey!" Benjamin cheered with excitement and spun her around. Looking into her amazing, sparkling eyes, he kissed her soft, tender lips ever so lightly and whispered, "I knew I found a jewel when I met you! I love you Mrs. Benjamin Robert Murphy!"

CHAPTER 48

BILL OF DIVORCEMENT

R akim finally arrived home and saw Deana sitting on the porch with tissues in her hand. He sat and stared at her wondering if she had received the call from their lawyer yet about the divorce. Suddenly, the kids bolted out the door running straight for him.

"Daddy! Daddy!" each of them yelled. He hopped out the car, hugged them tightly, and cried.

"What's wrong, Daddy?" Josiah and Jaheem asked.

He looked up and saw Deana run inside the house. "C'mon, guys. Daddy and Mommy need to talk to you."

When he opened the door, Deana was sitting at the kitchen table sobbing silently. He motioned for the kids to sit around the table with her. Breathing heavily, Rakim said, "Guys, Daddy and Mommy are going to take care of you in two different houses. It's going to seem hard at first but, you..."

"We are going to have two houses? Dinah asked sounding confused at first. Then she started clapping.

"Yay!" shouted the boys.

Deana was upset. "Children, settle down. Don't you understand? Your Dad is leaving this house? He's leaving us!"

Rakim shouted, "That's not true, Deana! I'm not leaving them—only you!"

Jaheem said maturely, "Mommy, I think it's cool we get to have two rooms. You said that you and Daddy would make sure that we are safe and happy. So..."

"Yeah, and we are going to see you and Daddy! Right, Daddy?" Josiah asked hugging him.

"That's right lil man. Your Mom and I are going to talk to someone about making changes so that you can take turns each week to stay with both of us."

"So, you're getting a divorce?" asked Jaheem.

"How do know about divorce, Jaheem?!" Deana glared.

"Well, Tommy, in my class, parents just did it and, he said that he gets lots of things since they divorced. He even has a second mommy."

Deana started crying again. Rakim told the kids to go to the den to play while he talks to Mommy.

When the children left, Deana stood up, slapped Rakim leaving a scratch on his face, and started pounding his chest.

"Stop it, Mommy! Dinah shouted. "Stop hitting Daddy!"

Deana stopped immediately as the boys returned to the kitchen. Embarrassed, she rushed over to Dinah to pick her up but, she ran past her to go to Rakim.

He picked her up and explained, "Sweetie, hitting is not okay. Now Mommy and Daddy will always love each other because we have you guys. We are going to work this out like adults. Your Mommy has a right to be upset with me." He turned and gently held Deana's hand. "But hitting is not okay. Right, Mommy?!"

"You're right. I apologize everyone. No one has a right to abuse someone; no matter how upset they are with them. Please forgive me for hitting you, Rakim. I'm sorry." He

hugged her and reassured her it was okay. Then, surprisingly he said to Deana, "I owe you an apology too. I'm sorry
for all the mean things I said and did to you and I ask you
to forgive me."

Everyone gathered in a circle and held hands. Dinah holding on—arms wrapped around Rakim's neck—would not
let him go. Rakim said, "We're going to have prayer before
I go."

After prayer, the boys eagerly left to play their video game.
Dinah finally let go of Rakim and asked him to read her a
story. He stayed with her until she fell asleep.

Deanna was in the kitchen cleaning up. He walked over
to her and took her by the hands. "Listen, Deana, I'm
divorcing you because I've been unhappy for a long time
and, I just couldn't live like this anymore. I didn't know
how to tell you I wanted out. It was tearing me up inside
knowing that I was hurting you by staying; so, I decided it's
best for all our sakes if I leave. The truth is, I don't love you.
You're a beautiful woman and a good catch—for someone
else."

"So, is that it? You caught someone else? Who's the fish,
Rakim?" Deana said angrily and pulled away from him.

"Please don't be like this, Deana. I'm asking the lawyer
for joint custody. I will pay for healthcare, daycare, and half
the mortgage. Look, you can go to work now...pursue your
dream job. Oh, and I'm giving you the Escalade and the
Benz. I'll take the Lexus and the truck."

She started pacing around the kitchen. "I guess I
should've chose Hasheem!" she lashed out.

"Um, I think he's chosen someone else." Rakim grabbed
some of his belongings and left.

Chapter 49

House Hunting

Damon went back to the hotel to change clothes. He has to meet the realtor from Royal Realty Properties at 1:30. Looking at his Rolex, he realized he had some time to kill; so, he walked down to the park. Nice restaurants—all types of food—everywhere! It was hard for him to decide what to eat; where to eat.

He saw an older couple sitting on a park bench and strolled over.

"Hi, it's a lovely day isn't it?"

Startled, the older gentleman stated, "It sure is young man."

He reached out to shake each of their hands. "I'm Damon."

"I haven't seen you around here before," the older lady commented.

"Oh, no ma'am. I'm in the process of relocation. Trying to find a place."

The older gentleman spoke up, "Young man, I apologize for our manners. I'm David and this is my wife, Florence."

"Pleased to meet you."

Looking him up and down, Florence admiringly said, "My, you sure are handsome and well-mannered. You married?"

Embarrassed and annoyed, David scoffed at his nosy wife, "Florence! Please forgiver her Damon."

"It's okay," he laughed and said, "I'm not Mrs. Florence."

"Not what?" She forgot her question.

"Married." Damon reminded her.

She looked at David and smiled. Acting as if he was upset with her, David rolled his eyes...then winked at her.

Damon checked the time again and realized he better hurry. "Do you know any good restaurants that have some good pizza?"

Unanimously, they said, "Santino's."

"Alright, I'll check it out! Thank you."

He made it halfway across the park and Florence stared with a smile.

When he arrived at *Santino's Pizzeria*, there was a long line. Glancing at the time again, he knew he wouldn't have enough time. So, he turned around and bumped into a couple.

"I'm so sorry; so sorry!" he apologized.

The man placed both hands on Damon's shoulders. "It's alright, man. You good?"

"Yeah, I didn't mean to bump into you." Damon said nervously.

Sierra reassured him they were fine. "No worries. Like my husband said, we're alright!"

Benjamin said, "Yeah, no problem." And gently slid his hands around Sierra's waist.

Damon's phone rang. "Well, enjoy your meal. See ya later."

He rushed over to meet the realtor, Mr. Watts. Pulling into the drive of the newly-built, two-story townhouse with a one-car garage. Damon smiled from Earth to Heaven! The realtor gave him the key to go inside to check it out.

He wanted to look around outside first and walked around the back to take a look. He overheard a man and woman on the other side at the neighboring townhouse talking about flowers and planting a garden.

When he followed the voices, his face became flushed and hot. He could feel his feet giving way as his body weakened.

Thud! Kaboom! He fell to the ground and, they came rushing over to his aid along with both realtors.

Damon tried to catch his breath as someone began giving him water and pressing a damp cloth on his forehead. Finally, coming to, they helped him to the steps on the patio.

Standing around him with frightened looks upon their faces, Mr. Watts, his realtor said, "You okay, Damon? Do I need to call the paramedics?"

Barely able to speak above a whisper, he managed to say, "Nah, nah. I'm okay. I think it's the heat."

The woman spoke using a motherly tone, "Young man, you should be careful. Is there anything my husband and I can do for you?" And she knelt beside him.

"No ma'am. I'm good." As he looked at James, his heart felt like something was pouncing up and down on it.

James knelt on the other side of him and kindly asked, "Damon, is it?"

Damon looked at him confused and said, "Yes sir."

Pastor Nolan placed his hand on his shoulder and asked, "Do you mind if we pray for you?"

Damon began to cry as he thought of Pastor Nolan's family and what Elliot had done. He said shyly, "Please do."

Surrounding him, including the realtors, Damon could feel the presence of God—the HOLY SPIRIT—taking away his guilt, shame, and past mistakes. Damon was set free—confirmation again. Everyone was in tears and hugging him. His heart didn't feel heavy anymore.

He looked at Mr. Watts and said, "I want this house!"

Pastor Nolan and Carol leaped for joy! They introduced themselves and James said, "Welcome, Damon. We're going to be good neighbors!"

Damon was excited, afraid, and worried altogether thinking, "We'll see once you find out I'm Elliot's foster brother!"

CHAPTER 50

RAYNA WONDERS

David and Grandma Flo were still sitting in the park when Ray-Ray walked up.

"Hey, sweetie." David got up and motioned for her to take his seat.

Grandma Flo hugged her tightly and, Ray-Ray cried in her arms.

"Oh, it's alright, child. God don't make no mistakes. Your Daddy ain't got to worry about them demons haunting him no more."

"I know, Grandma. But, I sure am gonna miss him."

"Of course, you are. He loved y'all so much, Ray-Ray. How Tasha and the twins doing?"

"They're okay. I'm more worried about Aunt Hilda."

"Girl, Hilda Mae gone be fine. She's a tough old bird!"

"Nah, Grandma, Tasha told me about how she has early stage dementia."

"I don't believe it. She'll be better once she come back here."

"Well, I think Tasha wants her to continue to stay with her and the twins. She wants to honor Daddy's wish of taking care of her."

"She ain't got to do that, Ray-Ray. Tasha still young and might want to get married again someday. Hilda Mae need to come on back here so, we can take care of her."

David butted in, "Florence, let them work it out. I understand—trust me. It's important to honor someone's wishes. Like..."

Florence grabbed him by the hand and said, "Yeah, like Harry's." And kissed him on the cheek.

Rayna stood and said, "Well, I just came to pack a bag and head on back."

"Why don't you stay with us and go back tomorrow?"

"Nah, Grandma, I want to see the twins as much as possible because when I get back," she paused and dropped her head, "When I get back, I got so much to do. I still have a job, you know." Wiping away tears now, she continued, "And I need to renovate my entire house. I don't want no part of Elliot around me."

David mumbled, "Or you could sell it."

"No, Granddad, I'm not going to let him take what I worked so hard to build! Elliot caused me to lose my baby!" Rayna sobbed. "I don't know if I ever will experience love...real love—a wholesome man."

David walked over and held Ray-Ray's hand, "Listen. You are still young and have your whole life ahead of you. When the time is right, God will send you who you deserve and that deserves you. Be patient, Ray-Ray. Take this time to heal."

Rayna leaned into him and sobbed uncontrollably. Grandma Flo reached in her purse and gave Ray-Ray some tissue. She squeezed her tightly and said,

"You fight for your life, child. It's yours. God gave it to you and with him backing you, you gone be alright. You gone be just fine."

"But, Grandma, I just don't want "a piece of a man" or "a half of a man." Elliot robbed me of my peace of mind. I don't know how long it's going to take for me to heal and get that back. Besides regret, hurt, and anger, I still have my house! And I'm keeping that!"

David reminded her, "Be patient, sweetie. Wait on the Lord."

After the hugs and goodbyes, she went home and packed a bag. Upon leaving, she saw a glimpse of Carol and James in the neighborhood walking alongside a handsome young man—as if they were helping him.

Ray-Ray thought to herself, "What they doing over here? And who is that with them? I'll find out after the funeral."

When she got back to Kelton, she noticed Tasha seemed a little distant. "You okay, Tasha, she asked."

"Yeah, I asked Aunt Hilda Mae if she would stay with us. She said she'll have to wait and see after the funeral. I was wondering if you could talk to her."

"Sure. Is she okay?"

"I don't think so, Ray-Ray. I walked past her room today and it sounded like she was having a conversation with Raymond's mother, Helen. She was telling his Mom something like, "I told you, sis, I'll take care of Raymond; he's fine.""

They both hugged each other and cried. Just then the twins came around the corner. Latisha said, "Y'all don't have to keep crying. Daddy's okay now."

Anthony handed each of them some tissues and smiled, "Now dry your weeping eyes, ladies because we are hungry." They all burst out with laughter.

"Okay, knuckleheads," Tasha said jokingly, "I'll order some pizza. And look we got to get some shut-eye. Tomorrow will be here before you know it."

CHAPTER 51

THE FUNERAL

The next morning, everyone was getting dressed for the funeral.

"I don't want to wear a stupid tie," Anthony argued with Aunt Hilda Mae.

"Stand still, Raymond, and put on this tie!" she shouted.

"I'm not Raymond, Aunt Hilda, I'm Anthony." He looked into her weary eyes and felt sorry for her; then, he let her help him with the tie and gave her a hug.

Latisha was giving Ray-Ray a hard time. "I don't like this hairstyle, Ray-Ray. It makes me look like a kid!"

"You are a kid, Tisha! Sit still!"

BOOM! BOOM! BOOM!

Frustration was written all over Tasha's face when she opened the door with one shoe in her hand and the other one on her foot, "What is it?" she yelled.

"I'm sorry, we just wanted to let you know the car is here," the mortician driver said.

Tasha was so embarrassed and apologized to the gentleman.

Then everyone started piling in one behind the other. James and Carol, Benjamin and Sierra, and David and Grandma Flo.

They gathered in their cars and followed the directions of Williams Funeral Home Services.

Upon arrival at the church, it wasn't as many supporters as Tasha and Ray-Ray expected. There were a few neighbors from their neighborhood, some of Tasha's former coworkers, some of Rayna's coworkers and friends, Latisha and Anthony's teachers and Principal, and church members she didn't recognize. For a second, Tasha even thought she saw Hasheem. Another stranger was in the parking lot blasting country tunes on an old pickup truck.

As she entered the church grasping Anthony's hand, she felt a sudden breeze that quivered her spine. That feeling of eyes watching came over her. She quickly looked around but saw unfamiliar faces.

"You okay, big sis?" Anthony sounded uneasy.

Ray-Ray quickly hugged him and said, "I'm fine. No worries."

The choir sang a couple of hymnals. Tasha, Carol, and Ray-Ray said a few kind words about Raymond. Saying goodbye to Raymond was not as detrimental as Tasha felt it would be for her and her three children: Latisha, Anthony, and Rayna. They all placed a red rose over his heart; except Aunt Hilda Mae. She refused to go to the casket.

When everyone was walking outside to go to their cars, a stranger walked up to Rayna and said, "Remember me?"

She gasped as if a ghost appeared while he grinned from Earth to Heaven.

Rayna was stunned.

With widened eyes and frowned faces, everyone stopped and looked on.

A PEACE OF MIND IS BETTER THAN HALF A MAN

RUTH HAMPTON

RUTH HAMPTON WRITES, LLC

FOLLOW THE AUTHOR

You can follow Ruth "Goody" Hampton on social media platforms: Facebook, Instagram, TikTok, and LinkedIn.

Website: ruthhamptonwrites.com

Book Promotions: Contact Ruth Hampton Writes, LLC with a brief message via email at rhamptonwriter2023@gmail.com if you want her to attend a book signing and/or speak about the book(s).

Her notable writings include:

- Christian literature: "God is Calling, Please Answer";

- Christian Romance-Suspense novel (Trilogy):

1. "A Peace of Mind Is Better Than A Piece Of A Man"

2. "A Peace of Mind Is Better Than Half A Man"

3. (Part 3 coming later)

Afterword

How Come?

Christian Romance-Suspense novel (Trilogy):
  (1) "A Peace of Mind Is Better Than A Piece Of A Man" (Part I)
  (2) "A Peace of Mind Is Better Than Half Of A Man" (Part II)
  (3) Part III coming later

The trilogy continues to bring awareness to the seriousness surrounding toxic relationships and domestic violence on various levels. The author base these novels surrounding not only from her past experiences but, also, for unalive, past and current victims concerning this. Far too long victims suffer in silence instead of holding their abusers accountable. Mainly out of fear and/or being alone. No one deserves to be punished verbally, physically, emotionally, socially, and/or mentally in any way, shape, form, or fashion by the one(s) they entrust their lives to.

Be empowered. Be inspired. Just BE!

If you feel you are in a toxic relationship or domestic violence relationship, please seek professional help. If you are an abuser and/or is abusive (without being physical), please seek professional help.

Disclaimer: The author is not a counselor, psychotherapist, psychologist, or any one of the medical field, nor does she claim to be. Be persuaded by your own mind.